Also by Andrew Craig

Unknown > Known (Poetry Collection)

After the Structures Collapsed (Poetry Collection)

A Shadow In Error

Andrew Craig

e-Book ISBN: 978-1-7644544-3-8

Paperback ISBN: 978-1-7644544-2-1

First printed 2026.

Printed in Australia.

A catalogue record for this book is available from the National Library of Australia

Day One

Rita Allen

There are times when darkness minds its own business and stays out the way. Doesn't draw attention to itself. Keeps its thoughts to itself. Makes sure the shadows stay hidden.

This is not one of those times.

The body had lain, where it was found; for at least a few hours. There were no maggots, at least not yet. There were signs insects and maybe a bird or two had begun using the body as a source of food. Later, it would be found that the body had been dead for an hour, at most, before being found. Naked. Beaten. Bruised. Bloody. That was never a good start for a live body, let alone a dead one. This was no accidental death. There were no stray drops of blood leading to the body. No scuff marks on the concrete indicating a struggle. No broken windows in nearby buildings. No stolen cars. Nothing to indicate this scene was where the murder took place. The body had been killed somewhere else and then put where it now lay.

A forensic investigation team were taking pictures. Gathering evidence. Analysing the body. Getting fingerprints. Finding pieces of a puzzle. Trying to solve it.

A few curious onlookers watched nearby. Most people kept walking past. They had seen enough dead bodies in TV crime shows; they did not need to see them in real life.

Some journalists did what they did, one of whom we will meet later. Asking questions. Getting nothing back.

A homicide detective arrived on the scene. Detective Rita Allen. Crime scene tape was lifted by a uniformed police officer for the detective to walk under. Rita walked with a purpose, but in no rush.

She had done this a few times.

Standing over the body trying to figure out what happened was Dr Roger Benson. Forensic team leader, Roger was getting close to retirement age. He had worked the recent serial killer case which Rita investigated. Their working on another case together was no coincidence. Forensic teams and detectives often crossed paths.

Stopping at then crouching down to view the body, Rita asked - So what happened?

Roger replied without looking up at Rita - Male. Caucasian. Mid to late fifties. Possibly early sixties. Found about an hour ago. We got here twenty minutes ago. No signs of struggle at the scene. The body however.

Rita asked a follow-up question - Who phoned it in?

- A jogger out for their morning run. Didn't even hang around for questioning. Just phoned up, gave the address and then went back to running, Roger said while still looking at the body.

Rita looked at the body as well. She was horrified by the various and multiple injuries the body had sustained. There had to be broken bones. Missing teeth. Internal organs ruptured. The hair on the victim's head was matted with blood, which had now dried out and turned to a filthy dark red.

Rita, eager to get on with the investigation, asked - What's under the finger nails?

- Just dirt. No nails broken off suggesting what happened was either unexpected or they had submitted to a beating.

- You don't submit to something like this, said Rita - What about the skull, what wounds are there?

- Cracked skull at the back. Broken nose and jaw. A few teeth missing. Wound on the back of the skull looked like it was made with a baseball bat or some dense heavy curved object. Maybe a large crowbar. I can't be definite at the moment. I need to get the body back to the lab to check further.

- What caused the broken nose, jaw and missing teeth? The other wounds, what of them?

- Not the same object which damaged the skull. If I had to guess, it looks like someone kicked the victim in the face. Or stomped on them. Maybe punched, but the person who did that would have a broken hand from the violence of the wounds so I'm thinking more kicked or stomped. I'm certain the victim's internal organs have haemorrhaged or ruptured or torn, but I won't know for sure until the autopsy. The arms, legs, back and stomach of the victim all have bruises which look they were caused by the same object which hit the skull. The face, I'm leaning to kicked or stomped.

- Vicious, remarked Rita.

- One of the worst I've seen.

- Found any teeth around the scene?

- No.

- The beating happened somewhere else and the body brought here?

- Yes.

- Nothing accidental about this.

- No.

Rita paused. She had seen some violence over the years, but the victim here, something else was going on. Violence like this had emotion behind it but this was more than just asserting power or getting revenge. This was the perpetrator trying to communicate something. And to who? Why beat and incapacitate someone with a blunt object but then maim their face by kicking or stomping them?

The serial killer case Rita had just worked on had its share of violence. This was a level above that.

Rita saw the journalist we are going to meet later. The journalist waved, trying to get Rita over to them. Rita shook her head no and motioned to the ground where the body lay. The journalist nodded in understanding.

- Does the victim have any tattoos, piercings, scars or other marks?

- No piercings. Not in the ears anyway. Not anywhere else as far as I can see. Scars and tattoos, I don't know, apart from that one on the left arm between the wrist and elbow. I really need to get back to the lab here. The blood and bruising could be covering them.

Rita would have to wait which is the very thing no detective wanted to do.

- Wait on, said Roger, look at this. Is that a burn mark?

Rita leant over to view the burn. It was a circle with another circle in the middle. It looked like someone had heated a DVD or CD then pressed it into the victim to create a burn.

- That circle looks like a CD, said Roger.

- Maybe a DVD, replied Rita.

- It is possible

- When will you know?

- When I do an autopsy.

- You can offer nothing else for the time being?

Roger frowned in defeat; he wished he could offer more, instead stated - No. Not until I do an autopsy. As we think the actual murder scene is elsewhere, we don't have much at all. Just a beaten body with indications of severe violence. Let's hope the victim's prints can offer some answers.

- Yes, let's hope.

Rita thought about speaking to the forensic taking the photos but opted not to. There would be no answers from the photos until they had been analysed. Instead Rita thanked Roger and began walking back to the squad car. On the way Rita jotted a few points into a notebook. She glanced over to the journalists and the questions were already being yelled out.

- Who is the victim?

- What's the cause of death?

- Have you got any leads?

- Are there any suspects?

Rita stopped. The journalists stopped yelling. Rita thought about answering the questions. Opted not to and re-started her walk back to her car. The journalists started yelling again.

They would get no comments for the time being.

It was time to get back to the station. Get that autopsy. Get the photos analysed. Prints checked. Identify the victim.

Rita couldn't believe the violence the body spoke. The hair matted with blood was as thick as she'd ever seen. And the bruises. They weren't your normal yellowish bruise you get when you accidently bump into the corner of a table. These were dark red. Almost black. They spoke disrespect. They spoke power. They spoke pain. They spoke anger.

Rita hoped like hell this body was a one off.

It wouldn't be.

Chapter 1

My subconscious is my mortal enemy. If the sub-conscious even exists which I very much doubt it does. Novels that start with words are second on my mortal enemy list. However, I'm going to use words to tell my story because I read somewhere that most people generally don't understand pictures. But for those of you who can understand pictures, here is a picture about this story:

> **THIS IS LITERALLY A**
> **PICTURE OF THE STORY**
> **YOU ARE ABOUT TO READ**

Here we are in this whatever the technical word for reality is. If I had to be honest, I would probably lie about it. So I'm not going to be honest. I've lost count of what day it is. They've all merged into one singular entity. Everyday just seems to be the same. A symptom of the times we live in where everything all the time is exactly the same forever. Today being just another in a series of today's that are the same. The factory of life belting out today's day after day. Same thing with yesterday's. Same thing with tomorrow's.

To get more of an insight into this, I tried using the internet. But I don't know how to use a personal computer. Besides, I don't have any fingers to type with. Or any eyes to see what I am typing. I don't have a head for television. Or the Radio. Or the internet. I don't have a head for the novel either. Or a piece of art like a portrait. Or a caricature. I am unable to listen to music. Or look at a sunset. Or taste fine wine and food. Or smell French perfume. Or watch a movie. Or read a book. I don't have a head at all. Or arms. Or legs.

This is why I'm not speaking. Or writing. Or walking. I do, however, have a headache. Or a broken arm. Or a punctured lung. I am having trouble locating the exact origin of this pain. If it has an origin. It might not. Which wouldn't be surprising. It's just there. Or it's somewhere else.

If I was a character in the novel you are reading, and I'm not saying I am but I'm not saying I'm not; I would be doing what I am doing now.

All I am is words on a page. A magic trick. An illusion. Or something else.

I am one of those people who does not forget but cannot remember. Or does not remember but cannot forget. Or just forgets. Or only remembers. Or something. I'm fairly certain I'm not sure. And even then I still have my doubts.

Sometimes I like to do things. Other times I like to not do things. It really depends on a whole of lot of criteria I am not aware of. Or maybe I am aware. How can you really know either way? No need to point out the things I do or do not do. I am well aware of what things I am doing or not doing because I am the person either doing or not doing those things. I will also deny doing or not doing any of those things that I am doing or not doing. Perhaps. I'm not committing to anything.

Here are almost 10 reasons why I am not going to write a list:

1. I do not want to
2. The formality of a list is intimidating
4. I like disorder
3. Lists are very predictable
6. They are unbalanced
7. Recording is an out of date process
8. (*Insert your own reason here.*)
9. Narrators run out of reasons
10. (*Insert another of your own reasons here.*)

I plug into digital social anxiety devices when required. It usually isn't but I do it anyway. No emotion exchanges, only information. The pieces break into smaller pieces. Crumbs. Then the crumbs break into smaller crumbs. Dust. Then the dust breaks into even smaller pieces. But I don't know what to call them. Small particles maybe. Transparency is a conspiracy. The human eye cannot focus on small particles. The human eye cannot focus on nothing at all. It doesn't really matter at this point. I could all but guarantee that when Albert Einstein was thinking about relativity, he wasn't thinking about any of this.

I'm not making a list but here is a list of things I need to get from the shops today:
1. Food
2. Other non-related food stuffs

I suspect that you think that is not much of a list and you're right. It is not much of a list. So what I am going to do is make more detailed lists.

Let's start with the food list:
1. Non-fresh food
2. Fresh food

And now for the other non-related food stuffs list:
1. Cleaning products
2. Products that are not cleaning products

Yes, I think this is some sort of game. But maybe it's not. Yes, I'm making this up as I go along. What were you expecting? Some realist manifesto? Some emotional rollercoaster? Some narrative arc which gives a heightened sense of verisimilitude? There is, and that is if there is, an answer to those questions, whatever the answer is, I can confirm and deny. The author is dead and the reader is not far behind. Now I think on it, the reader died when the author did. What we have left is an empty page governed by meta-linguistic systems. Or meta-semiotic systems. Or meta-narrative systems. Or some other type of system yet to be identified. I'm stuck somewhere else. Or I'm not stuck at all.

This story is not about you.

Let's expand on the non-fresh food list:
1. Food that comes in a box
2. Food that comes in some sort of plastic wrapping
3. Food that comes in a can

4. Food that comes in a jar

And the fresh food list:
1. Vegetables
2. Fruit
3. Bread
4. Meat
5. Dairy products

This is the cleaning products list:
1. Products that clean in the kitchen
2. Products that clean in the bathroom
3. Products that clean in the laundry
4. Products that clean elsewhere around the house described in
chapter two

And, finally, the non-cleaning products list:
1. I actually don't need anything that can go on this list at the
moment. I don't need alfoil or garbage bags or whatever else. But
maybe I should get some just in case I run out. I will decide later
when I am at the shops. And if I do, I will create another list then. Or
I won't and if I do that I won't get any of the stuff I would have put
on the list. (Make note to self: add shaving razors to shopping list).

Okay, next. Or whatever comes after next.

First up, the food that comes in a box list:
1. Cereal

2. There are other types of food that comes in a box, such as muesli bars or crackers, but I don't need them, so they are not going on the list

For food that comes in some sort of plastic wrapping, this is the list:
1. Pasta (Yes, I know that some pasta comes in a box but I only get the pasta that comes in some sort of plastic wrapping)
2. Salt and Vinegar flavoured chips. I also like barbeque flavour but I am getting salt and vinegar flavour
3. Chocolate biscuits
4. That's I all I need in this category

As for food that comes in a can, I need:
1. Tomato soup
2. Chicken and corn soup
3. Baked beans
4. Green peas, unless they come in a different colour and I'm 43.7% certain they don't

Not much food comes in a jar, but I need:
1. Strawberry Jam

Now for the main stage fresh food list, first up is vegetables:
1. Potatoes
2. Carrots
3. Swedes
4. Turnips
5. Parsnips

Fruit consists of:

1. Apples
2. Pears
3. Bananas
4. Mandarins are out of season so I'm not getting any of these

Bread is not much of a list:

1. Loaf of bread

Meat:

1. I don't eat meat so there is nothing to add to this list

Dairy products:

1. Milk
2. Cheese for toasted cheese sandwiches. Eating cheese any other way is disgusting. Unless it's on a pizza, which I will allow.

Let's turn to the non-food related items list beginning with products that clean in the kitchen:

1. Sponges
2. Dishwashing liquid, I actually don't need this but I want to point out that a bottle lasts for a decent amount of time and you don't need to buy very often

This next list is for products that clean in the bathroom:

1. Soap

Products that clean in the laundry:

1. Clothes cleaning liquid is similar to dishwashing liquid in that you don't need to buy it often, but you do need to buy a little more often than dishwashing liquid. Nonetheless, I don't need any clothes washing liquid at the moment.

Products that clean elsewhere around the house described in chapter two is a bizarre list. I'm not sure what to put on it if anything, maybe some air freshener:

1. Air-freshener

I'm probably not going to buy air-freshener but I'll put it on the list regardless. Or with regard. I don't know anymore.

I also need some shaving razors. Which should probably go on the list somewhere but I can't be bothered figuring out where.

And that's it. My list is done. Even though I wasn't making a list to begin with. If you think this all sounds a little crazy. A little insane. A little bit outside the usual. Blame the narrator. I've met them. And they are a pack of clowns. More on the narrator is a minute.

Before we move on, I'll admit to making a mistake but I will not admit that I admitted to making a mistake. Also, this sentence clause and this sentence clause mean the same thing. It's really up to you so take some responsibility here.

I get in my van which I will not describe. I will describe my house but that is the next chapter or the one after, I can't remember which. I think between now and then other characters are going to speak. I'm not sure who is narrating my story. Or if it is being narrated at all. It might be me. It might be someone else. If I was the author or narrator, here is where I would insert a qualifying clause to the previous sentence. But I'm not so I won't.

1

The parents of Mitchell Winters, Annie and David, loved him dearly. Like most parents they lavished their love and attention on their only son.

Their only child.

Mitchell was nearing five and about to start school. Mitchell had enjoyed his time in kindergarten. Sure, there was that first day where everything was new and frightening. But Mitchell soon overcame that. He had made some friends and adjusted well.

Outside of kindergarten and after the working day had finished, Annie and David couldn't do enough for Mitchell. They would take him to the park. To the circus when it came through town. To the birthday parties of his kindergarten friends.

Annie and David loved being parents and were planning on being parents to another child very soon.

Today, Annie and David were taking Mitchell to the shopping centre to get some stuff for Mitchell's first day of school.

All three were dressed in decent clothes. Not Sunday best, but not cleaning the house clothes either.

David had checked the child's seat in the back of the car was secured properly. Annie made sure shoe laces were tied and house keys weren't missing. Mitchell made sure to keep his parents on their toes.

Just before leaving David got a call from his boss about a client they were on-boarding. David was an accountant and regularly got calls from his boss. Annie was a nurse. Annie also got calls from her boss to fill a shift for someone who couldn't make it in for whatever reason. This weekend, David and Annie were only taking calls.

David wouldn't be calling a client to reassure them all is okay and Annie wouldn't be covering a shift at the hospital.

David finished his call.

Nothing major, David's boss just wanted to be sure he was accessing the right client's account in the database.

They got in their car and went to the shopping centre which was a short fifteen minute drive. It was in walking distance, but with Mitchell, it was easier to drive.

He could be a handful at the best of times.

Their house was in a nice area full of other couples who had a Mitchell or a Sophia. Sometimes one of each. Sometimes two or more of the same.

Mitchell was excited. He was looking forward to his first day of school and playing on the play equipment with one of his friends from kindergarten.

They eventually made it to the shopping centre.

For Mitchell it felt like forever. He said so out loud and David and Annie smiled to each other.

David found a carpark a short walk away from the entrance of the shopping centre. Annie didn't mind, this amounted to exercise and David did not nearly get enough. Mitchell had enough energy he could have walked to the shops from the moon. Annie giggled to herself with this thought. David asked what's so funny. Annie told him and they both laughed.

They began the walk to the entrance.

David passed the car keys to Annie who put them in her handbag. David carried the re-useable shopping bags.

They both watched Mitchell bounce around the carpark.

David asked - Were we both like that when we were kids?

Annie said - Maybe. Probably. Definitely.

Mitchell claimed – I need a new school bag. And a lunch box. And new shoes. And a hat. And pencils and a pencil case. And a water bottle. And sun-screen. And a diary. And an iPad. Plus lots of other stuff. Maybe a new toy. Maybe two new toys.

Annie said – We could get some of those things today and the rest another day.

Mitchell deflated a bit, then realised that would mean another trip to the shop. He smiled immediately at that. What would he get today? He would leave that to Mum and Dad, they knew everything.

- Could I still get some lollies to have after lunch today?

Annie and David looked at each other.

- We'll see, said Annie.

- Could he get a new toy?

- Maybe another day.

Mitchell screwed up his face.

Just before the entrance Annie stopped to look at some nice jewellery in a window.

A young girl, dressed in the uniform for one of the phone companies that have a kiosk in the middle of the shopping mall, walked by them. Annie and David let her pass as they moved closer to the window of the jewellery shop.

David asked - How much is that going to cost?

Annie slapped him across the arm.

Annie looked at a few other pieces. David ran the calculations through his head.

More overtime?

A pay rise?

Maybe Annie was due a pay rise.

They would need to sort out the plans for another child.

David put his arm around Annie and tried to move on with the shopping.

Annie didn't budge.

David tried a little harder.

A smirk drew across Annie's face.

David smirked also - pick one and let's go.

- What about all of them?

- Maybe another day.

- Oh okay okay.

Annie and David turned to go into the shopping centre but could not see Mitchell. They walked over to the bin, he was hiding behind there. Waiting for his parents.

Mitchell had done this before.

Mitchell would always laugh when Annie and David found him. The prank seemed to make both Annie and David's hearts skip a beat each and every time Mitchell played his game of hide and seek.

Mitchell was not behind the bin.

Annie and David's hearts doubled their rate in an instant.

Annie looked around.

David did the same.

They both turned in circles to see if they could spot Mitchell. David ran over to some nearby cars and looked around and under them.

Annie started screaming - Mitchell.

Nearby shoppers noticed what was happening and started to

look around, not exactly sure who or what they were meant to spot.

A few metres of space separated Annie and David.

They looked at each other.

Both realised at the same time what was going on.

Mitchell was gone.

Natalie Fenix

I'm in a corner. I'm not sure how I got here. Coerced, perhaps. Pushed, maybe. Encouraged by who knows what. A sub-conscious process that took control during a lapse of judgement. Or, as a final option, the corner being the only spot left which wasn't filled by something else. I'm not sure what shape the room is. I look at the other corners. There are many. Each are empty. Except for one. In that corner, darkness escapes from a small crack. The more darkness that escapes the larger the cracks get.

There is light.

Yet the light is dim. Distant. Always just out of reach but not yet defeated. Overpowered by darkness, which draws me in.

Seducing me.

Asking over and over: Will you?

And I answer: I will.

Again and again.

A feeling of helplessness washes over my body.

I struggle to come to terms with this admission. It doesn't make it any less false. It does not make it any more truthful. A middle sightly closer to one edge than the other.

The dark, suggesting often: it does not mean anything.

I can't help but feel slighted.

I am unsure how to react to these provocations. I slide further through the crack.

The light not getting any brighter; but not as dim as it was. Still just out of reach.

Darkness. Food for the hungry or water for the thirsty. It lets me become the person I need to be in order to contribute to society. It lets me fill my soul with the goodness it craves.

Without it, I'm lost.

It's then, I realise, what I have to do.

And like Ulysses recounting his death to Dante and Virgil, the waves crash over me with a thunderous sound and a carnage that words won't justify.

Unlike Ulysses, my journey is only just beginning.

Don't be mistaken. This isn't the first time I've done what I'm about to do. The problem with what I'm about to do is that there is no reason for its existence. That it does should raise more questions than it does.

What is a society which lets actions such as these occur?

Reality forever laughing at its subjects. Never really knowing the answer itself. Only concerned with what happens; not what should.

I acknowledge that I need to do what I need to do. It doesn't get easier. It doesn't get more difficult. I've spoken to other people who do this kind of thing. They all agree that it is something that needs to get done.

So I'm getting it done.

Permission is not required.

To get it done something has to give. Parenting. Partnering. Friending. I might make the world a better place but I'm failing in other parts of my life.

To overcome this dilemma, I've been told to consider that the world will never be a fully realised better place. Better is a limited resource. Making something better makes something else less better. Power is about deciding what parts of the world will be made better and what parts won't.

I'm not the person who decides.

I'm the person who gets it done.

You don't know me but you've heard about me. I'm one of the faceless the bosses talk about at their media performance. The journalist's, whose performance is just as effective, writing about the performance not the words the bosses speak. The real story gets lost behind the performances. The meaning diluted by political needs. By cultural hierarchies. By social conformity. By reader interpretation.

What I make better should be made better.

What gets made less better you won't complain about.

There is a knock at the door. It's unwelcome but not unexpected. It gets me away from the corner of the room. The darkness follows. Or leads. It's role in this journey ambiguous. Undecided in whether it wants to help or hinder. Keeping the light just out of reach. For the moment it's just there.

Always asking will you?

As if it didn't hear my earlier answer.

I open the door. Standing there is someone familiar but I don't know their name. They stand there, waiting.

- Well? I say with an air of impatience I didn't mean.

- We got one. Kid gone missing. You need to come to the station, says someone familiar.

I see them in the lunch room and morning roll call on occasion. I can never remember their name. There is always a new officer, rising through the ranks. Getting commendations. Well dones and/or good job.

- That's it?, I say.

- Yes, they say.

- Why didn't you just phone?

- We tried; phone said it was either turned off or out of range.

- Anything else?

- Get it done, they say.

They walk away. I close the door. I breathe a sigh of relief but it's painful.

I pick up my phone and try to turn it on, but it's out of charge. I plug it in. Darkness makes its presence felt further. Screaming for nourishment.

If I am not going to do this; now is the time to get out.

The room empties of light.

I make my decision.

I'm not going anywhere.

Some of the light seeps back into the room.

I hear an echo: Come to the station.

A memory rises. A pink raincoat with a blue butterfly embroidered into the back. A sweet smiling little face. Giggling at something I don't remember.

The memory falls as quick as it rose.

For which I am forever grateful.

The memory ruins me.

Every time.

I need to figure out how to stop this memory rising. Not forget the memory, just put it somewhere else. Somewhere safe. Somewhere, that if I need it, I can recall it as required. I need to control the memory. Which is harder than it sounds.

Controlling memories is like controlling an earthquake. It's as though they just happen. Without warning.

At some point, this memory is going to rise at a difficult time. It's going to put stress on a situation and someone innocent is going to end up hurt

And as an earthquake often has catastrophic consequences, so could the consequences of this memory.

I need to get this organised as soon as possible.

A moment of reality hits me. I remember where I am. The dark needs feeding. It needs the light. Pieces not crumbs.

When I get asked to come to the station, and I get asked often, it's never for a good reason. It's never to celebrate a retirement. A birthday. Those are done elsewhere. The station is about the job.

I have to get on with my job. It's something that needs to get done.

I get what I need and make my way to the station.

I look forward. The road rises and curves and rises again. The end is out of sight. Just beyond the horizon. Out of view. Knowing full well it's got nothing to worry about for the time being. There are mountains to climb and bends to straighten.

Reality laughing a little more. A little longer. A little louder.

Light acting as the shadow of the darkness.

And like Ulysses, I crawl up the shore to the gates of hell.

Chapter 2

Yeah, I've had friends over the years. So what? Where are all your friends? My friends, they're here and then they're not. I don't keep track of them. They don't keep track of me. Which works well. Unless it doesn't. But that's not for me to decide. If it is, I'm not deciding.

I have a friend here with me now.

Before I met my friend at the shop there was a person standing in front of their car. The hood was up. I asked what was wrong. They said their car won't start. I asked them if they had turned their car off and then back on again like a computer. Their faced scrunched up and shook their head a bit then went back to figuring out what was wrong with their car. I kept walking. Some people just can't accept help when offered.

I also saw two women having a conversation. It is probable, or most likely very possible, they were not talking about me.

Where I live looks like this. It's a bricked wall domicile. I think the colour the bricks are called is red. It might be called something else in other places of the world. But I wouldn't know. I haven't been to other places of the world. Some of the brick walls have windows in them. All of the brick walls and windows are covered by a roof. I don't know what colour the roof is. There is a floor which covers the entire area which the brick walls surround. I don't know what colour the floor is either. There are several internal walls placed in a strategical way creating smaller rooms. Some of those rooms have further internal walls creating smaller rooms again. Those smaller rooms have no windows. The rooms with the smaller rooms inside them have had their windows blacked out. A black paint was used to do that. People can only get in these rooms if I let them. They can only get out if I let them. Sometimes I don't let people in or out.

My friend is in one of those rooms.

Except, I don't know how it was done seeing as I don't have hands or arms or anything like that. That pain is still there however. Perhaps I cut myself somewhere. I can't figure out where though.

All the walls on the inside have been painted. I'm not sure what you'd call the colour the walls are painted. Maybe white. Some of the walls have taps in them where a clear liquid is expelled. I'm told that liquid is called water. Sometimes it's hot. Sometimes it's cold. Depending on the tap that is used. There are also several places throughout where the water disappears. I don't know where it goes. I've never looked. Or maybe I did look and forgot. But I can't remember. Just as long as the water goes. There is a way inside at the front and a way outside at the back depending on which way you're going. Sometimes the front is a way outside and the back is a way inside. There is no garage. There is a driveway. Yes, a car is in the driveway. Or a truck. Or a Van. Or something else.

I don't know much about cars so I'm not going to explain that. I can say it is blue. Or maybe white. Or perhaps another colour. Maybe I'll

find out what colour my car is later on. There are four wheels.
Maybe five depending on other criteria like how well you can count.
Or what you consider a wheel is. There is a radio. But only AM. Or
FM. Or both. I don't use it much so I can't say for sure. It might have
a CD player. Or tape player. I don't think it can play vinyl. But I
don't have any vinyl to check. I don't have any CDs or tapes so I
can't check those either. I'm not a car person. I'm not a car at all.

I don't know why I told you that. I was pretty sure I wasn't going to
explain the car. I guess the narrator has other ideas.

Or something else.

2

Annie and David were shocked. They kept looking at each other. Mouths agape. Going to point a certain direction then not. Starting to walk one way then deciding to stay where they are. Trying to speak but unable. It's not that they didn't have anything to say. They just couldn't figure out what the most important thing to say was. There were thousands of thoughts. Appearing. Staying. Then finally going allowing for the next thought to fill that now empty space. A cycle that had no foreseeable end.

Some people asked them questions that seemed almost rhetorical.

- What happened?

- Are you okay?

They knew the answer but the answers seemed unimportant. What was important was finding Mitchell. Perhaps Mitchell had decided to take his little game of hide and seek that extra step. And if that was the case, young Mitchell was going to catch hell for this.

Right after Annie and David hugged and kissed him a thousand times each.

The shopping centre security guard was there. Asking questions. Which also seemed rhetorical. Not getting any answers from Annie and David. Well, none that made sense.

Some of the other shoppers speculated.

- Run over by a car one said.

- I didn't see a kid to begin with said another.

Confusion was in control creating further confusion.

The security guard asked - Has someone called the police?

There were no verbal answers. Some people shrugged their

shoulders

The security guard called the police.

There was a change in the air. A day that started out so bright had begun to darken.

The security guard walked over to Annie and David.

- You need to tell me what's going on. I need to tell the police.

Annie and David looked at the security guard. Then at each other.

Then David looked back at the security guard and said - Mitchell is gone.

Annie burst into tears like any good parent would. She fell to the ground. David tried to catch her.

He couldn't.

He fell to the ground as well.

He and Annie hugged. For a moment David opened his eyes and on the ground was a CD or DVD. Written on it was 'WATCH ME'. He briefly broke away from Annie.

Annie said - What? What is it?

- Over there, on the ground, replied David nodding his head in the direction of the CD or DVD.

Annie looked over as did the security guard.

- Leave it there, the police will be here soon, could be evidence, said the security guard. The security guard also wanted to say "CDs and DVDs always get found with 'Watch Me' or 'Don't Watch Me' written on them mostly kids playing jokes" but didn't.

David held Annie in his arms. The police will be here soon he thought. Whenever soon was which wasn't soon enough. Time takes forever on certain occasions. This was one of those occasions.

David kept hugging Annie. Annie hugged back. David was a good parent as well. He tried to keep it together.

He couldn't. His tears began to flow in time with Annie's.

The police arrived. The security guard pointed out the CD or DVD. One officer took a picture with their phone and put the CD or DVD in an evidence bag. Both Annie and David wondered if more pictures should be taken and finger prints dusted from nearby objects like the bin or the nearby bench.

David asked – Shouldn't you be taking fingerprints from the CD or the bin?

The officer thought about how they were going to answer and then said - No. We'll take it to the station, see what it is and then we will follow up if needed.

The officer was going to add "TV crime shows are almost never accurate when it comes to collecting and processing evidence", but thought better.

Like the security guard and through past experience, the officer thought it was most likely kids playing a joke. The officer turned away and began to talk to a group of people watching on. None of the people saw anything of note. Someone saw a person walking by but couldn't remember any features of the person. Another thought they saw Mitchell get into a car but someone else thought they saw Mitchell get out of a car. It was as though they witnessed what they thought rather than what actually happened.

The other officer stayed and spoke to Annie and David.

David spoke for them both - We were just looking in the shop window. Thirty seconds. When we turned around, Mitchell was gone. Thirty fucking seconds.

- Did either of you see anyone who may have seemed out of place?

The truth was Annie and David didn't remember anybody. They were keeping an eye on Mitchell and in the thirty seconds they averted their gaze, Mitchell was gone.

The other officer said – It would be best if you both came down to the station to state a full report detailing the event leading up to when Mitchell disappeared.

Both Annie and David looked at the ground. Living through it once was hell. Having to retell the story again would be torture.

The officer that was talking to the crowd walked over to the security guard and asked - Can the camera footage be handed over?

The security guard nodded and began the short walk to the security office. In the security office the guard started recording on a new machine. The guard stopped the old machine and rewound to the time Mitchell disappeared. The guard was tempted to watch the footage but decided that wouldn't be a good idea. Instead, the guard downloaded the footage onto a flash drive. The guard got a yellow envelope from the stationary shelf and put the flash drive inside and sealed the envelope. On the front of the envelope, in black texta, the guard put the date and the time. The guard walked back out to where Annie and David were.

During the walk, the guard wondered what secant line meant. Secant Line Exteriors. It's what the full title was. It was a plain graphic. Normal letters in black. No fancy font or picture of a paintbrush or hammer. Just the words. Phone number underneath. The security guard couldn't remember the number. Probably a painter or some kind of pergola or veranda builder perhaps. That was the name on the tradie van that almost knocked her over when she got to work this morning. Something to look up on the internet after work she thought.

She made it back to Annie and David. She looked at them both. Concerned with the way they both looked. She imagined the worst but couldn't quite understand how they were feeling. That feeling can only be felt by other parents who had a child go missing. She handed the envelope to the other officer then asked - Is there any more I can do?

There wasn't.

- No, another officer or detective would get in contact for further information if needed.

The officers, Annie and David got into the police car and began driving back to the station. As they were driving out the shopping centre carpark a TV news station van was driving in.

Annie and David looked at each other. How did they get here so fast?

The other officer said - The TV stations have devices which enable them to listen in on the police channels. They probably heard the words child and missing then a news producer would have decided to send a crew out. Someone decided yes in this instance.

The other officer was a little surprised it was just the one TV news station van. Perhaps the others were just around the corner.

Annie and David weren't ready for what was going to happen next. They just hoped Mitchell was not hurt.

The security guard watched as they drove out the shopping centre carpark and the TV news station van drove in. If that kid wasn't found in the next hour or so, this would be on the news tonight. The security guard grabbed her mobile phone out of her pocket and called her boss. Something like this, needed escalation, supervisors needed to be made aware and paper work needed to be filled out documenting the incident.

The guard had a feeling the kid wasn't going to be found in the next hour or so. Chaos was about to descend on all involved. More media would likely be involved. More police. Well intentioned citizens. Self-absorbed attention seekers. Among others.

The guard thought about Mitchell. She hoped he was alright.

He wasn't.

Rita Allen

Rita waited at her desk at the station. The desk was mostly empty. A photo of Rita's family sat off to one side. Stained coffee cup, currently empty, was placed just in front of the photo. A couple of pens were scattered across the desk. Two screens and a docking station waited for Rita to plug in her laptop. There was a desk phone.

Rita had no evidence which could make her hurry off to find a suspect. Not from the scene. What was that burn mark about? The visual images of the body popped into her mind. She hadn't seen a body that beaten and bruised for a bit. She thought when the last one that bad was but couldn't remember. She waited for the forensics to sort out what they found. She watched other detectives go about the station. She saw uniformed police officers do the same. She saw people, who were arrestees or witnesses, move around the station. It looked chaotic, but ordered.

Walking by her desk was the other detective Rita had worked with on a few cases. Detective Natalie Fenix. Usually when there was some overlap between cases like when a parent had murdered their partner and hid the children somewhere. The children, usually, were with a relative. Rita did homicide, Natalie did missing persons.

Rita got along with Natalie. Sometimes. Rita also didn't get along with Natalie. Sometimes. Two very different ways of going about it, but when they worked together, it was as if they complimented each other. Cases got solved which is what the bosses wanted.

Rita, steady, confident, collaborative, had a family and had a determination to get the right result. Natalie, a little dark, tragedy in her past, preferred working alone but near on a genius and a savant for solving puzzles. Natalie was the kind of person who could complete, in a short amount of time, a thousand piece puzzle where every piece was the same colour.

Rita thought about relationships between detectives like this on TV crime shows. Only some of it was right and most of the time it just made people think they were experts in crime scene analysis or court room procedure. TV crime shows seemed more of a caricature of police work which made the characters in the shows almost cartoonish.

Rita didn't watch TV shows like this.

Rita's boss knocked on her desk. His name is Detective Inspector James Rawls.

He had a career. Worked through the ranks. Solved some major cases. Sorted out some administrative issues which saved a lot of money. Is, no doubt, on the list for running the whole show someday.

- Who's the body?, asked Rawls.

- Don't know, waiting on forensics.

- Burn mark on the body in a circle? Possibly a CD or DVD?

- Yes that's right, how'd you know?

- Called forensics to see what was going on. They told me.

- Oh, yes, burn mark could possibly be a CD or DVD.

- A CD or DVD with 'WATCH ME' was found at the scene were a child went missing this morning. I'm teaming you up with…

Rita cut in before Rawls could finish his sentence.

- Aren't these CDs or DVDs usually just a joke from some kids. What else links a missing child with an unidentified body?

- I'm about to go speak to Fenix to tell them to team up with you.

Check this CD and DVD thing out while we wait for forensics to process the evidence. If we don't look at the CD and it turns out it is linked, the media will have us on a stake.

- Ok.

- What do you need to get this body to turn from red to black?

- The usual, first, the victim identified. Second, a murder scene established. Three, a suspect, or suspects, located. Fourth, evidence linked to a suspect. Five, arrest made.

- Murder scene?

- Yes, the body was murdered somewhere else and put where it was found.

- Forensics didn't mention that. For now, give me a minute. I'll get you teamed up. Check out the CD or DVD. The parents of the missing child will be here shortly. Speak to them. Hopefully, forensics will find something and we can go from there.

- Sounds good.

Rawls walked away. All Rita could do was wait. She looked at the clock. She watched Rawls walk into his office with Natalie Fenix following him in.

She straightened up the pens on her desk. Where they were scattered, now they were in a neat group. Red on the left. Black in the middle. Blue on the right.

She looked at the clock again.

A few minutes had passed.

She looked at her family photo. Smiled.

She looked at the clock again.

Only another minute had passed.

Rita waited some more.

Chapter 3

This new friend of mine.

Will.

Not.

Shut.

The.

Fuck.

Up.

Always carrying on about something. I'm not sure what something is. I say hey friend how about you help me out here and define something. This new friend, stops, thinks and after a brief pause, goes back to not shutting the fuck up.

My new friend is getting boring quick.

I tell my new friend I don't have any games. Or any TV. Or any iPad. Or radio. Or newspaper. Or books. I tell them I can move stuff with my mind but only when people aren't watching. I ask my new friend if they can read. Judging by the response the answer is no. Or maybe it was yes and they are lying.

I tell my new friend that vampires suck. They're always the top of the monster chain. But there is nothing scary about them. Seriously, how fucking scary can a monster be if you can defeat it by throwing a piece of garlic bread at it? Vampires are so shit.

My new friend doesn't laugh. Or maybe they do and I just don't know what laughter is. This is all too confusing. My new friend says some things. I don't know what they mean. It's as though they just learnt how to speak but can't say any words properly.

I walk out the room and into another room. I wish I had sound proofed the smaller rooms. Maybe I did and I just haven't realised it yet. Blacking out the windows was a good idea. Sound proofing them as well would have been a better idea. When I go into the other room there is no noise except silence. If that even makes a noise. I've never heard it. It's got to be a better sound than what my new friend makes. I'm going to listen to this for a bit.

I feel hungry. Or maybe it is another type of feeling. Maybe it's not hunger at all. Maybe a bug flew into my eye. Or out of my eye. Or my eye is a bug. Which explains the term bug-eyes. I'm pretty sure my eyes aren't bugs. Maybe my arms and legs are bugs. Which is impossible seeing as I don't have arms and legs. I think I feel hungry again. Feelings are confusing.

For now, I have other things to worry about. I have a heap of groceries from the shop I need to unpack and put away. There is an order I do this but the order is different each time I put the groceries away. It's hard to explain. If I could explain it. Which I can't. So don't ask me to.

I tell my new friend I've met people who like to speak about themselves in the third person. I find it very irritating. Or I would if I existed. But seeing as I don't I'm not irritated at all. Unless this is the pain that I've been feeling. Not pain but irritation. It would make sense but I'm not going to explain it. Some things aren't worth doing. Like making sense. And if you're not going to do something you may as well not do something well.

Where was I?

Right, people who talk about themselves in the third person. I like to talk about myself in the second person. I recommend doing this when talking to someone else. They have no idea what is going on.

Here's an example in film script form, as told in the second person:

EXT. – Afternoon – Side of the street

You
Hi, how are you?

You
Err, fine I guess?

You

What have you been up
to lately?

You
Are you talking to me?

You
Yes, I'm talking to you.

You
Not much. Just work and stuff.
Occasional venture outside to
find new friends.

You
Please be quiet. I am trying to
have a conversation with you.

You
With who? Me?

You
No. With you.

You
What?

You

Look, I'm trying to talk to you
but you keep interrupting.

You
This is getting weird. I'm
going to walk away now.

You
If you must.

You
What do you mean you?

You
You. What else does it mean?

You
You?

You
Yes, you. Can you please leave
you alone while I talk to you?

You
Okay then.

CUT TO:

And it can go on like that for however long a conversation like that lasts. Which is usually about as long as what I've shown. About 2 minutes 38 seconds if you want to be accurate. And you do. After that you walk away. Irritated; probably. Besides, based on what you've shown, it could be irritating for you. But how can you be sure? It might be pain. Actually this is getting confusing for me. I don't know if I'm talking about you or you.

My new friend is wide-eyed. Not saying a thing. Shaking. Muttering words like Mommy. Or Daddy. Or please. Or leave me alone. I ask my new friend if they are hungry or thirsty or something else. My new friend says thirsty. I point to a cup of water. My new friend says hungry too. I point to a packet of chips.

Can I go now my new friend asks?

I laugh.

Nope.

I get up and leave the room made up of small rooms. I think I'm feeling hungry again. Or thirsty. Or both. It feels like something else. Maybe I'm just confused from talking about yourself in the second person.

I finish putting the groceries I got earlier away.

Natalie Fenix

I sit opposite my husband. The other parent to our kids. I need to tell him what I am going to do. Last time we spoke we agreed that I wouldn't do what I'm about to do anymore. We have a daughter about to start school. Paying off a house. That whole bit.

The darkness is an addict screaming for one more hit.

And it will not stop screaming.

- Hi, I say.

- How are you?, he replies

- I have a job to do. Perhaps for the last time.

He asks a question.

- That is not what I meant.

He asks another question.

- I just need to do this one last time.

- Things can't keep going on like this.

I agree with him.

- What can I do to help?

I have no answer.

- Will this be the last time?

I say - I'm certain it will.

There is a moment of silence. The silence says he is happy to hear it will be my last time but unsure of the truthfulness in my statement. He's heard statements like this before.

A box is opened. Life pours out. The box is closed. Darkness pours out instead.

I say - There is still light but it is almost gone.

- I don't want that.

- I don't want that either.

He asks me one final question.

- I hope not.

- Our daughter is about to start school. First day is a fortnight away.

- I'll be there.

- She's looking forward to it. She misses you. I miss you.

- I miss her. I miss you to. I miss… (my voice trails off).

- I know. I do to.

- I got to go.

He says, with a sense of resignation but not finality - Look after yourself.

- I'll try.

I grab my badge. My gun. My keys. I look at a picture I keep in my pocket. I don't know how many more times I am going to be able to do this. That memory. Each time I look at the picture. Another small cut. Not painful, but there. The small cuts building on top of each other until the amount of small cuts can no longer be ignored. This time I can keep the pain down. Eventually the pain will prevail. Pain knows this and remains patient. Biding its time. Waiting for the perfect moment to strike. I can't let it win. I focus on the job at hand. On what needs to be done.

I need to figure out how to control the memory.

I shut the door behind me and head to the station.

When I get there my boss, Detective Inspector James Rawls tells me - We need to have a word.

We go into his office.

Rawls starts - This is gonna be quick, I got a meeting to be at five minutes ago.

- It's me. Letting you know it's my turn. Last time, I respond.

- Going around again? Thought you might. I'm teaming you up with Rita Allen.

- Teaming me up, you know I work better on missing children cases alone. I don't…

Rawls cuts me off - Last time? You said that last time. And the time before. Probably the time before that to. Anyway, new events have taken place and you need to work with Rita on this. You've worked with her before and the results were just what we needed. We need those results again.

- I can guarantee you, this will be my last time.

 I am one hundred percent confident of that, however, the tone of my voice suggests otherwise.

I continue - I know me and Rita have had some success, but, when I am on my own, I can just get on with it. Follow-up where I need. Speak to who I must. Get it done.

Rawls stares at me, not in a bad way, more of a 'are you finished?' way.

Then he says – You're working with Rita. Body found with CD or DVD burn marks. Your case, a CD or DVD with 'WATCH ME' written on it found. Sounds like it might be a connection between the two. Find out. Figure it out. Get it done.

- Body?

- Yes, apart from the burn marks, I have no other details. Oh wait, body was dumped there. Actual murder happened elsewhere. Speak to Rita. Sort something out. Get it done.

- Ok.

- You talk to your husband before coming here?

- Yes.

- What did he have to say?

- With all due respect Rawls.

- Yes, I know, none of my business. But I can't have a detective going out, dealing with these types of crimes with their head in another place. What the fuck did he say?

I pause.

Then I say - This has to be the last time or it's finished for us. Kid starting school. They miss me. They miss us. All that type of stuff.

- And you said what back to him?

I look Rawls in the eyes - I told him this is my last time and I miss him.

- This job takes more than just a respectable effort.

- I've been doing this now four years.

Rawls knows this.

- Still, no harm in letting people know where you are at. Speak to them. Hear what they have to say. Never know, they might say something that will save your life.

- Weren't you were supposed to be at five minutes ago? - I say with maybe a little more spit in my voice than was intended.

- You done?

- Yes.

Rawls doesn't say goodbye. Just leaves and goes to his meeting. I sit alone in his office. His desk is untidy. The walls have merits, commendations, medals, badges, and pictures. I think about staying on and earning those accolades for myself. Then I think no, not for me. I leave and go to meet Rita. I see her. It looks like she is waiting for something.

Detective Rita Allen. Parent of twins. 10 year old twins. We've worked on and off for three years now. Rawls is right, we do work well together. The other detectives question why one of us hasn't moved over to Homicide or Missing Person's. They've seen the level of understanding we have of each other. Some of our more cynical male colleagues make jokes about sisters sticking together or female intuition. They ask us if our husbands know how well we get on with each other (they do).

Or some other made up patriarchal shit.

Neither Rita or myself can be bothered making a complaint.

Fuck them.

Truth is if something goes awry in this workplace you need someone who can anticipate your next move. You need to able to anticipate their next move. The type of people we deal with, you need to win at all costs. They won't stop trying. Ever. It's win or die for them. And that's no understatement either. The people we deal with, winning for them may mean dying for us.

Which we cannot let happen.

- Rita, I say.

We shake hands.

- Hey, teamed up again.

- Yep. Get it done.

- Get it done.

We go to Rita's desk. Rita sits in front of her two screen setup and says - Still waiting for some forensics to come in about the body this morning. You know much about it?

- No, just the burn marks and that the body was dumped where it was found.

- Yep, waiting for forensics. This the last time?

- Yes.

- Last time you said that was the last time. This is the last time right?

- Yeah, probably.

- I know people who say that and before they know it they are retiring with a 35 year career and a pension for life.

- This is the last time. That memory I've told you about. It's killing me more and more.

- Death by a thousand paper cuts?

- Yes, but I'm way past thousand.

- You need to figure out how to control that memory. I've told you what works for me but my memories and yours are quite different memories.

I try to be convincing - I'm working on it but failing. I'm in a boat with a small leak and using a very small colander to bail out the water.

- Want me to get the department psychologist to call you?

- No. (I should have said "Fuck no")

- You sure?

- Yes, I'm sure.

- Seriously though, if I feel shit is getting out of control I won't hesitate to get you out. You hear?

- Yes, I hear. It won't get to that.

- Get that memory in check.

- I'm on it.

There's a brief pause in our conversation. We take a breath.

Rita says - So we have a missing child. CD or DVD found with

'WATCH ME' written on it. Body found with CD or DVD burn marks. Possible connection.

- We need to watch, listen, ingest, whatever is on that CD or DVD, I state.

- Who you looking at first for the missing child?

- I don't know, I say - I have a few people on my list. Not one of them will be looking forward to talking to me. You got a suspect for the body?

- No. At the moment, this is a worthy who-done-it. What about one Matthew Trenton, a.k.a. Trenchie?

- What about him? I blurt out, - What I mean is; do we call him Matthew, Matthew Trenton, Mr Trenton or Trenchie?

- We call any suspect or person of interest by their name. Knowing alias' is good, leave the nicknames to the street. Matthew Trenton is what we will use.

- Apologies, with cases like this, well, I get frustrated quick and when you know certain things about certain people it's hard to use their proper name, I say in an attempt to try to explain my actions. I've been doing this long enough to know better.

- I know. It's all good. We need to use proper names, says Rita.

- So, Matthew Trenton?

- I think he got out not long ago. If he got out. Word is he is trying to stay on the narrow.

- Un-fucking-likely he is staying on the narrow.

- That's my point, says Rita, - he's got a way in. Someone who is part of the puzzle but whose piece hasn't been connected to the other pieces yet.

- Matthew Trenton?

- Yep. Matthew Trenton.

- Perhaps we talk to the parents of the missing child before we start with Matthew Trenton. Watch this CD/DVD. That way we'll have something to talk to him about.

- Seems logical. Where are the parents?

- I'll find out.

I use Rita's desk phone and dial the main desk to find out where the parents are so we can talk to them. Rita puts the CD/DVD into an external drive CD/DVD drive on her laptop.

One of the front desk uniforms answers and says – the responding officers are still speaking to the parents at the station, you might want to get in here.

I respond with - We're already at the station and we'll be there very soon. Hang on a second.

It's a DVD, playing is a single static shot of what looks like the front of the TV Station. There are no people in the frame. No cars. There is no sound. You can see the shadow of a tree moving in the wind. Just a static shot of the front of the building. The angle looks up to the station giving it an authoritive feel. Like it looks down on us. Commanding. Deciding on everyone's behalf. Rita looks at me and we both furrow our brows trying to figure this out.

- Is this some kids playing games? I ask Rita

- I have no idea what this is. A TV Station? Found where the kid went missing?

- Yes, on the ground.

- I think we need to talk to the parents, maybe they saw who dropped it and can't remember at the moment.

- You still there?, I ask.

- Yes. We got security footage as well.

- We're on our way there now. Get the parents a coffee. Put them in an interview room. We'll be there very soon.

The light shines bright. Then the reality that security footage doesn't always show anything makes itself known.

The darkness laughs.

The bright stops shining.

I tell Rita - The parents are here and there is security footage.

Rita needs to take the lead on this.

- Rita, I say - you ask the questions.

A look of calm spreads across Rita's face.

But what the fuck is the TV station thing about?

3

At the police station, Annie and David sat in an interview room. Each holding the other's hand. A constable had offered them a cup of coffee when they arrived and they said yes. The coffee cups sit on the table in front of them; neither cup being sipped from. The coffee just sits in the cup. Cooling down. Ready for its ending when it gets poured down the sink.

They had only been in the interview room for ten minutes but it felt like ten years. Annie held a tissue dabbing the tears from her eyes. David didn't have a tissue but he had tears in his eyes. Both wanted to be out looking for Mitchell. Both knew the intelligent thing was to talk with the police, bring them up to speed and find Mitchell. The conflict of wanting to follow instincts versus doing the smart thing was ruinous. Both knew the initial twenty-four to forty-eight hours was crucial. Mitchell had to be found as soon as possible. The longer it took the greater the chance of failure.

A couple of detective's entered the interview room. Annie and David, although not showing it, expressed some relief. Finally, something was getting done. One of the detectives spoke. The other took notes and listened.

- Hi, I'm Detective Rita Allen. This is my colleague Detective Natalie Fenix. We have a few questions to ask but before we do, can I get you anything?

Annie and David shook their heads. No.

- Okay, I think the best place to start was this morning.

Annie and David both took a deep breathe. David started - The morning began like most Saturday mornings; with Mitchell running into our bedroom waking us up asking for some breakfast.

- Every Saturday morning, added Annie - he couldn't do it through the week. Me and David both get up early during the week to get ready for work.

David kept on - So we got up, got Mitchell breakfast and then we made some for ourselves and started packing stuff to go to the shop.

Rita asked - Does anything stand out over the previous days? Seeing unfamiliar cars regularly? Maybe a person you've never seen kept walking by your house? Phone calls? Expected mail not showing up? Any out of the ordinary events?

Annie and David thought for a moment. And then a moment more. But nothing seemed to stand out. No strange cars. No strange people. They barely got any letters these days, everything was done via email. If any mail got stolen it was probably just catalogues for the local supermarket.

- So you got up, got breakfast, got ready for the shops and then what?, asked Rita.

It seemed obvious but Annie said it anyway - We went to the shopping centre.

Rita looked at Natalie. They understood Annie's response and why she said it. But it wasn't what they meant. There was a silent agreement between the two detectives to keep going forward.

Rita pressed on - Did you notice any car following you?

- No.

- You didn't get into a road rage like incident while driving to the shops?

- No.

- What about when you got to the shop, notice anything there?

- No.

- So you got to the shops, then what?

David answered - We parked the car. Got Mitchell out the back. Grabbed some reusable shopping bags. Locked the car and started walking to the entrance.

- Does anything stand out there?

- No. Everything just seemed normal. We looked in a shop window for thirty seconds and when we turned Mitchell wasn't there.

- You noticed Mitchell was not there and then what did you do?

- We looked behind bins, under cars, around corners; everywhere. But we couldn't find him.

- Did you hear a car speed off? The screeching of wheels after you noticed Mitchell was gone?

- No. But to be honest. I don't remember hearing anything, said David.

- Neither did I, Annie agreed.

- What about the DVD?

- It's a DVD is it?, asked David - I wondered what it was going to be. What's on it?

- I can assure you nothing graphic nor nothing criminal. Just a static shot of a building.

- What building?, Annie asked with anticipation rising in her voice wondering if that was the building Mitchell could be in.

- It's of a TV station, that's it. It's like one of those time lapse shots. A long time shown over a sort amount of time. Everything moves fast but the building just stands there. Shadows move across the building quickly. People are there for a frame or two then gone.

- David, you saw the DVD on the ground?, Natalie asked.

- Yes, that's right. Just near the bin. I must have looked over, around and under that bin a hundred times looking for Mitchell but didn't see that until the police got there.

- Didn't see who put it there?

- No.

Rita looked at Annie who shook her head no.

- Is it true a dead body was found this morning?, Annie asked.

- Yes.

- Could it be related to Mitchell going missing?, Annie asked further.

- Possibly. We don't know yet. We are waiting the results from forensics. We will know more when we hear from them. That should not be too much longer.

Rita and Natalie didn't have much to go on. Annie and David being unable to offer anything helpful. Maybe the security footage held some important lead. Some information pointing a certain way. Even a crumb. Just to get them moving.

Annie and David sat in silence.

Those coffee cups still untouched.

Annie asked - What can we do now? Go home? Wait here? Go look for Mitchell?

Rita responded saying - Go home. If we have any questions, we'll call.

Annie and David got up.

Rita remembered - Do you have a picture of Mitchell?

Annie looked into her purse and pulled out the picture of Mitchell handing it to Rita. There is a brief pause. Nothing said. Not verbally. Not physically.

Rita, sensing a good point to stop the questioning - Please go home. Stay by the phone. If we have a question we'll call. If we have any information to give. We'll call. If you remember something, have questions, anything, please call.

Annie and David nodded.

Rita pointed to a uniformed police officer - He is one of our media consultants and he'll escort you out.

Annie and David start to walk out the police station. Their car still at the shopping centre. It was going to be there for a while. Home would have to wait. As they were walking to the exit of the police station they could see a group of people standing out the front. A couple of those people had cameras on their shoulders.

The media.

Supposed bastions of free speech.

Truth tellers.

Entertainers.

Annie and David held hands. They looked at the media throng.

A nightmare was coming to life.

They both clenched each other's hand tighter.

Ebony Bowen

I've wanted to be a journalist for as long as I can remember. Other kids, when they were ten years old, they were using a hairbrush as a microphone singing into it and thinking they were their favourite popstar. I used the hairbrush for a microphone as well but I used it to conduct interviews with my family. My younger brother and sister got sick of the interviews after a while. My sister went and pretended she was a popstar. I was able to get my brother to pretend he was a camera person. Then he got bored and pretended to be his favourite sports star.

I went through high school where every assignment was written like a newspaper report. Even the maths assignments. The teachers talked to my parents a few times but I got through high school. Went to university and spent most of my weekends at home reading about the industry. The ethics. The law. The process. I couldn't get enough. Graduated and got a junior position at a television news show. Worked my way through the hierarchy. Started off as a researcher. Then a writer. Then a producer. Then got given a chance to work my own stories. For some reason I loved the police and crime news. Going to the scene. Going to the police station. Going to court. Trying to piece it all together before the police could. To get that scoop. The thrill of the chase the police call it.

Every now and then getting a story was like walking through mud. You had to keep walking. No matter what appalling fact you discovered while researching the story. It all had to be written about, with taste and reason of course. Leaving anything out was lying. For a journalist lying is worse than giving up a source. Which means we do neither.

Ever.

My news director, Dennis Rucci, comes over to my desk. He's older. Kids moved out of home with their own families. I think he is just seeing this through until he retires in a few months. There is a glow behind his eyes but the fire went out years ago.

- Did you hear the police channel a few minutes ago? he says.

- No, I reply - I was in the archives.

- Ahh, the archives room. I remember when that room had order.

- I don't.

- Nevertheless, the police channel. A child has gone missing from the shopping centre.

I look at Dennis - Parents freaking out?

- Yes. What of the body this morning? Heard anything else with that?

- All I have so far, is a body was found. So far unidentified. Possibly killed in one location and put there.

- So not some random mugging on the street gone wrong?

- Sounds it. Got to wait for the police to identify the body. They haven't as yet.

Dennis mulls things over. Gets around to asking - So what's taking them so long to identify the body?

- Insert any number of prearranged excuses here.

- Geez, ain't you fun.

Dennis smirks. So am I a bit. Dennis kind of nods towards the door - Go find out about this missing child. See what the parents say. If anything. See what the police say. If anything.

- Ok.

It's always concerning when parents aren't losing their minds when their child or children go missing. Most times it usually means they had something to do with it. Bit like when the police have no main suspect so they always question family first when someone is murdered.

- Where are the parents now?

- I expect they're at the station. Doing what they can, says Dennis.

- And you want me to go and find out?

- That is what I asked.

I put my pen in my top left shirt pocket. Grab the coat off the back of my chair. My notebook off the desk. Take my phone of charge and head out to the police station.

As I'm walking out Dennis yells - Get a camera person and production truck. I got a feeling this is going to escalate fairly quickly.

Dennis hasn't said something like that for a little while. In the past when he did, he was usually on the money. Perhaps one final push before retiring. I go to the tea room. I see Cary Deakins staring into a cup of coffee. He is thinking about something but I'm not going to ask. We have history and we made it clear to each other to keep it professional when at work. I walk up to him and look at the cup. It's filled with coffee. Its swirling like someone is mixing in milk except the coffee is black.

The coffee swirls.

- Want to work this story with me; we got to go over to the police station for a start?

Cary looks up – Yes.

Natalie Fenix

Rita asks - Matthew Trenton or security footage?

 - Footage.

We make our way to the AV room. Rita sits behind a table, puts a notebook in front of her, gets a pen ready for writing and waited for the footage to begin. I plug the USB into the wide screen TV. I grab the TV remote and select USB port one and press play.

Nothing plays. My heart skips a beat. Did the security cameras not get anything? I check the TV. The USB is in port two. I update the TV settings and press play.

The screen lights up.

For all the advances in video capture, recording and playback, for some reason, security cameras still have that grainy aesthetic. They still only record what was in front of them. Some people walked by. Some cars drove past. I fast forward. People walked by quicker. Cars drove by faster.

Rita says - Stop. Play from here.

I stop the fast forwarding. After a few more frames have passed the moment we want to see arrives. We see Annie, David and Mitchell walk into frame. Annie and David walk over to the jewellery store. Someone else walks behind them. Not sure who that is, maybe a shopper. Could be an employee, they look like they are ready to work not shop. Mitchell looks away from them. It looks like he begins to laugh.

Rita goes - Did Mitchell just laugh then put something by the bin and walk away?

I rewind the tape.

Yes, Mitchell laughs, drops something by the bin then walks off camera. As it stands as of now, that is the last time anyone saw Mitchell.

Rita asks - So what did he laugh at and is that something that was dropped the DVD we just watched?

I say - I have no clue. There is other footage from other cameras. Let's see if they show anything else.

We watch the footage from other camera angles. They all show the same thing. The family walking into frame. Annie and David going over to the jewellery store. Mitchell laughing, dropping something, possibly the DVD we just watched, by the bin then walking away.

I ask - Did he get into a car? I can't see anyone walking with a child.

Rita replies - We have to think he got into a car. If we don't see anyone walking around with a kid, then a car must have been used.

No car being visible makes what we are doing just that little bit harder. Time is not what we have. We watch the footage again. And then again. Nothing stands out.

- Now what?, I ask knowing full well the next step.

We both sit here. Thinking. Neither of us have time to do this. Not for long anyway.

Rita says - We need to get this footage to analysis. Confirm it was this 'Watch Me' DVD Mitchell dropped by the bin. We need to read the notes from the other officers who took statements from people who were at the shopping centre. We need to go through the list of people recently released from prison who have some sort of affiliation to child abuse, kidnapping, anything like that. If someone has stolen a car and they were recently released from prison, we need to talk to them. White collar criminals are included in this. Who knows what kinds of things they get up to when they aren't ripping people off. We need to start dotting our I's and crossing our T's. Do not give the media or some politician a point to score on.

I agree with everything.

- What about your body from this morning?, I ask Rita.

Rita weighs it up, - Fuck it, she says - a missing child who could still be alive tops an unidentified body. We get any more bodies though, then we may have to rethink things.

Seems a reasonable point. The missing child should be the priority. At least for the time being. I'm sure there are parents everywhere saying the missing child should be the priority no matter what else. Which is also a reasonable point. But politics, and the media mainly, do like spinning crime into some advantageous event they can profit off. A mad serial killer is made for TV entertainment. Missing children or not, fear of the unknown makes people choose some very strange things. Like putting some TV influenced serial killer above the wellbeing of a missing child.

We need to start getting some leads. So far the DVD, security footage and parents have not given us much to go on.

I volunteer - I'll start on the recently released list.

Rita nods, says - I'll get this USB to analysis. Gather the other officer's notes and go through them.

This was, and still is, our usual routine. Get information. Process. Make a plan. Go through plan. Amend plan as needed. Get more information. Repeat.

There was one thing that needed to be done but neither of us wanted to do. We have more important tasks to do. We have to speak to Rawls, get him up to speed. I mention this to Rita. Eventually I give a begrudging nod - I'll do it.

Rita nods back. She grabs the USB. Puts it in an envelope and walks to the analysis section.

I gather my thoughts. Speaking to Rawls is like speaking to the media. Every word potentially has the opportunity to be completely mis-interpreted. I knock on his door.

- What?, says Rawls with about as much charm as a welcome mat.

- You finished with your meeting?

- Yes, what is it?

- Spoke to the parents. Got Nothing. Watched the DVD found where the child went missing. It's a static shot of the front of the TV station. Watched the security footage from the shopping centre. Got nothing.

- So now what?

- Rita is taking the USB to analysis and going through the notes of the officers who spoke to the people who were there when Mitchell got taken.

- Mitchell? That's his name?

- Yes. Mitchell Winters.

- Okay. Just want to get it right. No doubt there'll be a media session about this.

- I can't speak on that but yes; no doubt.

- Media. Worse than talking to your boss.

I don't say a thing. I certainly agreed.

- Forensics got back to Rita with anything?, Rawls continues.

- Not so far.

- Ok, so what're you doing?

- Giving you an update and then going to check the recently released list.

- Recidivists. I would not be surprised if it was one of them. What is it with some people who go to prison that they have an incredible need to go back?

- Darkness is addictive.

There was a brief pause.

- TV station you said?

- Yes. Not sure what it's about. Might be some kids playing games. The security footage did show Mitchell dropping something by the bin, where the DVD was found, before walking off camera.

Somethings up here. Rawls is staring at the ground, thoughts off in the distance. Face lost some colour, I ask Rawls   - TV station got some dirt on you?

- No, no. Just haven't had anything like that before.

Rawls is deep in thought. Maybe memories from an old case. A bad case. Or worse, an unsolved case.

I need to get on with my job, I ask out of courtesy - Anything else?

Rawls doesn't say anything, just walks to his seat and sits down and starts typing on his laptop. I leave and shut the door.

I go to get a list of recently released prisoners. Surely something will show up there. I get the list and go to my work station. The first name I see on the list is unmistakable. It confirms Rita's thoughts from earlier.

How do some people get out of prison?

Rita gets back to our work station. I look at her and say one name.

- Matthew Trenton.

Chapter 4

Groceries are away and my new friend is as well. I don't mean away away. Not yet. Maybe later. Depending on which way things go. If they even go a certain way. They might not go at all. They might stay static. Still. Not moving which is what still means. But I think we're a little away from being at that spot.

But you never know.

I'm standing here. That lull between doing one thing and then doing another. Do I get another friend for my friend? It's never ending. You get one friend. Then you need a friend for that friend. Then a friend for that friend. Then that friend needs a friend. And so on and so on. Before you know it you have no room for new friends so old friends have to go away. Then you get another new friend and then an old friend goes. And so on and so on. Or something. Or something else.

It needs to stop somewhere.

Maybe draw a line in the sand. Or write a line in the sand. Whatever. I don't know. What the fuck does a line in the sand do anyway?

All words are meaningless when you think about it.

Someone calls me on my phone. I tell them to shut up with that shit. I don't need to hear it. Or I do. Someone tells me I do need to hear it. Which makes it easier for me. Making decisions can be very decisive on occasions. So I hear it. I say I have nothing to do with that side of things. There is a reason I keep myself away from other self's. Away from the Circles. Someone says who said anything about the Circles? I say I thought that's why you're calling because the Circles told you to. Someone says the Circles don't exist and if they did they sure as hell didn't tell me to do anything. I say sure, someone like you thinks for themselves. There is a silence. I laugh. Someone says you finished. I say I think so. Someone asks did I do it? I say what? Someone goes you know what. I say alright, what if I did? Someone says I can't keep doing that. There is more on the line now. Someone tells me whatever I did I need to have not done. Which is strange to hear. How do you not do something you've done? I tell that to someone and they say well unfuck it then. I ask someone who they are. Someone tells me I know who they are and to stop playing games. I tell someone something. Someone goes you have until my next phone call to not do whatever you've done. I ask someone when will the next phone call be? Someone says they're not sure. I say ok. Someone ends the phone call. Or I do.

I'm not sure.

Between you and me, someone can get fucked. I'm not doing anything that fucker said. There is a reason I don't run in the Circles. When you have a circle inside a circle inside a circle it's like a list. The outside circles are the unimportant parts of the list. The inside circles are the important parts of the list. And I fucking hate lists. So I'm staying away from the Circles.

I go down and ask my friend what they think of the Circles. They just say I want my mommy. Which is pretty disappointing. I ask again, this time with a bit more force. My new friend starts screaming. I did make this part of the house soundproof. Or maybe I didn't. So although I can hear my new friend scream no-one else can. Or maybe they can. It's like my new friend is in outer space. Except they're not, they're right in front of me. I tell them to shut up. They scream louder. I tell them to shut up and this time I say please. They keep screaming.

I pick-up the crowbar I have leaning against the wall next to the door and start hitting the door of the room my new friend is in.

I scream too.

Loud.

My friend keeps screaming and crying. I hit his door louder and scream. My new friend stops screaming and looks at me. I stare at him. Angry that I had to do that. I tell my new friend don't ever do that again. My new friend keeps looking at me. I say don't do that again. Okay? My new friend nods his head and crawls to the corner of his room. I nod my head.

I put the crowbar next to the door where I picked it up from. I notice some blood stuck to the crowbar. It looks like some is on the wall. But I don't know how it would have got there unless someone put it there. Some flakes of dried blood are on the ground from when I just hit door. It could be my blood but it isn't because I don't exist. It could be someone else's. If they even exist. But how can you tell? It's not like I can do a blood test to find out.

I say hey.

My new friend looks at me.

I point to the crowbar.

I walk out the door.

Rita Allen

Matthew Trenton. We like him for a few we haven't solved in homicide. If not him, someone he knows. I couldn't believe when I heard his name. He should be in jail for life. But, I don't know, society has this thing with giving people a second chance. That's all good, but you shouldn't get a second chance to hurt a child, or kill someone or any number of other things. Having some awareness of who he is, I don't think Matthew is our murderer. But we won't take any risks. We'll still ask some questions even if it is cross someone off our list. I still have my doubts that the body from this morning and the missing child are linked. Then again, I have worked cases were they were linked with even less and more dubious data.

The world grows and evolves.

Crime does too.

Forensics. I wish they'd hurry up. My mobile rings. It's them.

- Rita Allen.

- Some news. Perhaps good. Some bad, says Roger.

- Good first.

- We have cause of death.

- Cause of death is blunt force trauma leading to a cracked skull and bleeding on the brain?

- Yes.

- The way the victim was bloodied and beaten it couldn't have been anything else.

- We checked under the finger nails, there was nothing. Either assailant cleaned them or the victim didn't see the oncoming attack.

- Maybe the victim just new there was no point in fighting. Were there drugs or alcohol in the victim's blood?

- Small amount of alcohol. Maybe one drink at the most.

- A final shot of some sort of spirit before the spirit leaves the body.

- Sounds possible. Until we find a murder scene or murder weapon we can't know for sure.

- Ok, so now the bad.

- Yes, the bad. Victim's prints aren't in our fingerprint database. There was no ID or anything in the victim's personal effects. The burn marks found on the body, probable cause is a CD or DVD shaped object. Running their blood now through the database. Maybe there is a match for that in some previous case. It will take an hour, maybe more.

- The waiting game again.

- Nature of the business we're in. Until then, I can't give you anything else I'm sorry. The security footage is being analysed now by a colleague. Based on their initial viewing notes, nothing stands out. Can confirm the child dropped, what we now know is, the DVD next to the bin before walking off camera. Got a list of visible plates. Will send over to you so you can go through. My colleague will watch a few more times, if anything else seems pertinent we will let you know.

- Yeah, it was a DVD. You told Natalie yet

- Was about to call, thought I'd bring it up as I know you two have teamed up.

- Yeah, don't bother, I'll let her know, she's here with me now.

I put my hand over the phone and mouth 'DVD' to Natalie. She nods. Writes something down in her notebook. I glance at the pages. There are scribbles all over the pages. Notes. Pictures. Diagrams.

Looks like there is torment in her thoughts. With her past I'm not surprised.

I tell Roger - Alright, let me know if anything comes up.

The call ends. It's nice to have some threads forming. Mitchell dropping the DVD suggests the TV station has some meaning or context to his disappearance. The victim's lack of defence wounds suggest he either was ready for what happened or was accepting of what did happen. Burn marks probably caused by a CD or DVD, still a distant link, but perhaps the body and the missing child are linked.

- The TV station means something or has some relationship here?, asks Natalie.

- Yeah, I don't know how we get a foot in the door there. TV stations always on about freedom of speech until it is them who have to do the talking. Then all of a sudden it's no comment or speak to our lawyers or come back with a warrant.

I think we need to speak to Matthew Trenton. Seems the most likely suspect at the moment. Has form. No stretch of the imagination that the next step in his crime growth is murder or manslaughter. I'm just about the say let's go speak to Matthew when I hear a familiar voice. On the TV are Annie and David.

We both focus on the TV and hope to hell they don't say anything they didn't tell us.

4

There were a handful of journalists, from TV and newspaper, but somehow they made enough noise that all other sounds were drowned out. The Uniformed Police Officer escorting them out tried to make a path for Annie and David to walk through but each time a space was made a journalist would fill it.

The journalists all asked questions at the same time.

There was no order.

No hierarchy.

Only chaos.

- What happened?

- What do you remember?

- Is there anything you'd like to say on camera?

- Can we get a picture of you two in front of the station?

The questions went on and on. Each journalist basically repeating the other journalist's questions.

The Uniformed Police Officer, trying to gain some control and create a sense of order, spoke - More information would be passed on to the press as we get it, for now please make way and let these people leave.

Journalists, however, used to this behaviour from pretty much everyone, ignored the Uniformed Police Officer's pleas and kept filling the newly formed empty spaces and asking even more inane questions. Annie and David stopped walking. This had to be dealt with now because no way were they going to be strong enough not to lash out later. David held his hand up motioning for them to quiet down. The journalists kept asking questions. David kept his hand up and after a minute the journalists got the point. When they stopped

David lowered his hand.

The Uniformed Police Officer started talking - This morning, about ten am at Colehaven Shopping Centre, Annie and David Winters were doing their weekly grocery shop. With them was their son Mitchell Winters. Mitchell Winters is now considered missing. Both Annie and David have been assisting investigators with their inquiries. Annie and David have provided a picture to us, but at this time we cannot disseminate that photograph. We will send a copy to your stations and office shortly, but we need to get our reporting done. We need to document any statements made. We need to put into evidence security footage from the shopping centre. Please give us time to get this information sorted. For now, we cannot elaborate further. If you are prepared to do this in an orderly fashion, Annie and David may be prepared to answer questions.

The Uniformed Police Officer looked at both Annie and David who both nodded in return. The journalists took turns asking questions. David answered them all. Annie holding David's hand. Tight. Their hands had that pink/white look hands get when they've been holding something for a long time.

- What does Mitchell look like and what was he wearing?

- Mitchell is five years old. He is about waist high tall. Brown hair. Light brown eyes. He is wearing a grey jumper with cartoon characters from the Regular Show on the front, green pants and black Adidas sneakers. As the police just said, a photograph will be sent to you shortly. If anyone has any information, please call the police. We hope Mitchell will be found as soon as possible. We do not want to move to offering a reward but we will consider if and when that time comes.

- What were the events leading up to Mitchell's disappearance?

- We got to the shop. Got out the car. Started heading to towards the entrance. We stopped to look at something in a shop window. It must have been only for twenty to thirty seconds. When we turned back around Mitchell was gone.

At that last bit, David's voice cracked a little. He thought he was going to breakdown. A question from another journalist brought him from the edge and he was able to hold it together.

- What about suspicious cars?, asked one journalist.

- People?, asked another.

We don't remember any suspicious vehicles or people. Nothing out of the ordinary. Nothing that stood out.

- Is there a chance Mitchell might have just walked away and is lost?

- No.

Here the Uniformed Police Officer interjected - We have watched the security footage and we are confidant Mitchell didn't walk away on his own voluntarily.

- Was there a car? How do you know he got into a car?

Again the Uniformed Police Officer answered - The cameras didn't get what car, if it was a car, Mitchell may have got into nor did it capture any pictures of the person or persons who have taken Mitchell.

- Is there anything you want to say to the person who has Mitchell?

Annie answered this question - Please let him go.

Sensing now was a good time to end this, The Uniformed Police Officer asked – Are there any other questions?

There weren't.

The Uniformed Police Officer spoke with finality - For now if you have information call the police otherwise let the police do their work. Please respect Annie and David's privacy. Both are in a state of shock and need time to process what's happening.

Annie and David didn't disagree. Throughout that whole time their hands remained joined. The Uniformed Police Officer advised Annie and David to go back inside the station to wait for the journalists to leave. Annie and David didn't argue. It was a good point. They went inside.

David asked Annie - Should I call someone to get us?

Annie replied - Call a taxi.

So David called a taxi.

Ebony Bowen

Neither the parents nor the police gave much away. Just what we already know. A child is missing and if anyone has information: call the police.

Cary is putting the camera away and the sound equipment.

He says - Didn't give away much did they?

- No they didn't, but maybe they don't know much at the moment, I reply happy Cary is at least talking to me.

- They always know more than they're letting on.

- What do we do now?

I know the answer, we need to go to the shopping centre, talk to the security, maybe there is someone still there from this morning, maybe contact my police friend. This is more to keep a conversation going with Cary. He hasn't said much to me since, well, since.

- Let's go get a few shots of the shopping centre. While we drive there, call your police friend, see what they have to say.

- Sounds good.

I nod and get into the passenger seat. Cary closes the van door, gets in the driver's side, starts the van and starts heading towards the shopping centre.

I get my phone out and call Detective Rita Allen. I tried talking to her this morning about the body. She had more important things to do which she showed by motioning to the body when I tried to get her attention. I need to ask her if the body from this morning and the missing child are linked in anyway. I first met Rita while doing my journalism degree. She was a guest in one of the classes and we've remained in contact ever since. Rita gave us tips on how to interact with police when investigating a story. There seemed to be no right way to go about it. Develop a relationship, ask your questions and hope you get an answer that will make your story. The underlying principle is that the police want control of the investigation and how the story is reported. The police will only give information when, and only when, they want. Which usually means their side and that of the victims is under-reported. The story always ends up with a this-is-what-happened-and-that's-all-we-have-for-the-moment style. I always hear from the parents asking why more information is not being disseminated by the police. The answer is always the same: you don't want to give out the only clue which might catch the perpetrator. It's frustrating for everybody but the logic behind it all is sound.

I call Rita. The phone answers.

- Rita Allen

- Rita, it's Ebony Bowen.

- Ebony, how goes? Got to be quick, I'm in the middle of something.

- Mitchell Warner, got any information?

- Thought you might call about that. I don't. I can't say anything further. Weren't you there just then when the parents spoke?

- Yeah I was. You working the case? What do the police know that the rest of us don't?

I have to least try to get some further information.

- Yes and I can't say. Quote me and I'll deny.

- Are the body from this morning and missing child in anyway linked?

Rita doesn't say a thing. She knows the game. Probably why she was at that journalism class. I would not be surprised if certain police get nominated by senior police to help out at journalism school and 'get to know your local police' type events. Maybe that's being cynical. Perhaps not.

- Rita?

- I'm here. There are very vague strands which could be used to suggest a link. However, and I stress the however, we have not verified a link at this stage. We have nothing else and are continuing our investigation.

- Will you call me when you get something?

- Depends what we get. Who we get it from. What it's about, says Rita

- Alright. I'm going to keep digging.

- If you find anything that could progress this case you'll let me know before you go putting it up on the news?

- Depends what we get. Who we get it from. What it's about, I reply.

A moment of silence.

Another moment of silence.

Two in a row is never good.

Rita eventually says - If you get anything run it by me first.

- Is that a question?

- No. Got to go. I'm where I need to be. Talk later.

I've got more information from brick walls than that.

- Your friend much help?, goes Cary.

- Not at the moment.

We sit silent. It's not uncomfortable. Waiting to get to the shopping centre. I look through the window of the van at the oncoming traffic in the other lane. Something is in the distance and its energy is starting to be noticeable.

It's a little concerning.

Natalie Fenix

Darkness illuminates the sky further. It's a grey hue. I can sort of see where I need to go. It's a matter of moving that way without being made to go another. Not to let influence push you off course.

Its somethings that needs to get done.

It's not that the people I have to interact with hold their cards close to their chest. It's that they don't pick-up the cards to begin with. Trust is something these people do not have. If somehow they manage to find some, it will certainly not be shared with someone like me.

Rita drives and stops the car in front of Matthew Trenton's house.

I've met the journalist she was just talking to, Ebony Bowen, but we've never had a full conversation. It's as though all of people in the detective pool decided Rita would be best to speak to journalists and give them tips on how to interact with the police. The senior officer agreed. Ebony has asked me some questions on previous cases but I don't give much back. She noticed. Now, Ebony tends to speak to Rita only. Though, we might need Ebony later so I shouldn't do anything to put her off.

- If we need your journalist friend, we can depend on her later?

Rita shrugs and says - Probably, I've known her since her university days. We've remained in contact ever since. She's a good kid.

- How often do you deal with her?

- A couple of times here and there. If she needs info on management changes or something like that I don't help. She was ahead of me one time. Was waiting there for me to make an arrest.

Don't know how she found out. Didn't ask. She didn't tell.

- What about this time?

- With what we know at the moment, I don't think she'll be getting to far in front. Let's go speak to Matthew Trenton. See what this he has to say for himself.

- This is not going to be fun, I say.

- These people give me the creeps. It's the kids I do this for. Them or the families of the deceased. Which reminds me I need to follow-up on some things after this. Remember to remind me.

We park in front of the house next door to Matthew Trenton. No curtains move. No-one peeping out from a window. They never do in suburbs like this. It's like keeping your own business is a type of self-preservation. We get out the car and walk to the door.

I knock.

Once.

Twice.

Then an answer.

- Yep?

- Hi.

- The fuck you want?

Rita, beginning to stir the pot, says - Let's start this again. Hi.

- Fuck you to, what d'you want?

- An answer.

- Yeah? To what fucking question? What the fuck are youse going to ask that I can answer?

- Good point, I say.

- Fuck both you dickheads.

The door shuts.

Rita says, almost as though to herself - When will people learn? She knocks on the door.

- Open up Matthew. We're not leaving. You know we like you for some murders.

Rita keeps knocking. She's done this before. She won't stop until the door is opened again. Longest its gone is 2 minutes and 17 seconds.

From the other side of the door we hear - Those bodies aren't mine. I keep telling you I have never killed anyone.

- But there is always a first and what do you know about those bodies?, says Rita.

I'd give you some insights into Matthew Trenton but there is really nothing insightful to offer. Bad parents. Bad childhood. Bad choices. No siblings. No friends. No education. Wrong side of the wrong side of the tracks. Police file that has about three volumes.

43 seconds the door opens.

- Close the door again and find out, I say.

- Alright then. Ask your fucking question?

I say - We're looking for someone.

- So who is it?

I get the picture of Mitchell Winter's from my notebook and pass the picture to Matthew. He takes it. Looks at it.

- I told you last time I'm into that shit anymore. Trying to move forward and all that good get out on parole shit. I don't need you here. Ever.

Sometimes you come across people who make you think if things went a little better earlier in life then who knows what they might have invented. Cured. Solved. Fixed.

Matthew Trenton is not one of those people.

- Picture doesn't look familiar, says Matthew

He stares at it a little longer than necessary. I hold my hand out to get the picture back. He passes it back but doesn't take his eyes off it until I put the picture in my pocket.

I ask - You know who might of?

- All the people I used to know have gone to jail or are dead.

There's a small pause. I have no questions. Rita has no questions. Matthew has no answers. The silence makes me feel uneasy. I look around. Something isn't right here. Matthew picks up on it.

- Bit nervous hey?

- What've you done?, I ask.

Rita puts her hand on her gun.

- Nothing. Yet. But if something happens a friend will not hesitate.

- Hesitate to do what?

- Screw you over. Fuck! Did you really think I live here alone without some sort of safety net? You've fucked me over already. I don't need that shit again.

- You have no safety net. No-one is going to look out for you no matter how much you pay them. Who has Mitchell?, I demand.

- Yeah, that's what I'm about, telling you who they are. I'll tell you about the picture. Then I walk back inside and after I've shut the door. You can leave.

- So tell me about the picture.

- I don't know who that is. Never seen them. But I have heard.

Rita interjects - Heard what?

- Let me finish. Fuck. I've heard that there is a newbie on the block. Not a newbie, but, ah, that's all I'm sayin'.

- Who told you that?, I ask.

Matthew looks at me as if I can't figure it out why my question isn't being answered.

- I don't know who it is, he goes - don't think they are from around here. Don't know where they live. Like I said before. I'm not into that shit anymore.

Rita asks - So who does know?

- Maybe.

- No.

Now I know what the something not right feeling is. It always gets worse before it gets better.

- No what?

I say - No, not them. They are worse than you when you were at your worst.

Rita goes - It's not who I'm thinking about is it?

- Yes. It's them. Why didn't you just go there to begin with?, Matthew questions.

I say - Because Matthew, your name was first on the list of recently released. Not his.

- It's them or this is where it stops for you. Now I'm going to go back inside. Once the door is shut, then you leave.

The door shuts.

I look at Rita and she says - At least we got some answers.

- Not the ones we need.

Rita says - We've got less and still won.

- I'm not sure how we're going to find the person we need to find..

I get the picture of the kid out my pocket. The memory rises. I push the memory down and put the picture back. A second of silence screams out. I take a deep breath. The silence screams further. I'm not sure how to stop the screaming. I'm not sure how to stop the silence. Both in an eternal war for dominance with everything else having to deal with the consequences.

And the guilty? These people. These crimes. They are like a circle in a circle in a circle. Like a target. And like a target, those on the outside, are expendable, easily caught and don't really know anything about those further inside the circles. Those further inside the circle. The mister or misses untouchables. Less expendable. But are the ones who commit the heinous acts. The ones the TV reporters like to investigate but don't have the courage to describe with accuracy or honesty. The ones where, if they do get caught, their identity is kept secret in case it influences the juries. The ones where no light shines on them. Even the darkness despises them.

And after the waves crashed over Ulysses' boat, killing him, a bigger wave came eroding all traces of its crime.

The crack in the corner of the room opens a little wider and the darkness escapes just a little more.

This is killing me.

Rita says - We go straight there now?

- Yes, I say - Right now. You have to follow-up on some things, so I will drive.

- That's right. Thanks for the reminder.

5

Annie and David waited for the taxi. They watched the journalists begrudgingly going back to their vans and packing up their cameras. Writing down that final thought. That sentence which might make the story but would probably be edited out by the editor. That clip which wouldn't be aired. Every now and then a journalist would look over debating whether they should ask one more question or get one more picture. None of them did. Eventually they all left to try and make a story for the evening news or tomorrow's papers. Content with what they had. Knowing pushing a bit too far could result in even less information later on. They seemed disorganised but it was part of the way the profession operates. They would wait for the police to send through their report, the picture of Mitchell Winters and then go from there. Annie and David stood there watching.

Waiting.

Annie spoke - I never want to go through something like this ever again.

David agreed.

The Uniformed Police Officer waited with Annie and David then asked - Do you want a coffee or water or something?

David replied for both Annie and himself - No thanks, the taxi will be here soon anyway.

The Uniformed Police Officer followed-up - We'll be in contact with an update later. Here's your taxi.

Annie and David walked out to the taxi and got in. Gave their home address. The driver tried speaking but Annie and David only gave short answers. Not in a rude way but the taxi driver knew the signs of people who don't want to talk and just drove to where he was told. From station to home took about twenty minutes. David paid the driver. They went inside. They noticed how different the house felt without Mitchell. It was as if the house lost its soul. Its identity. Its heart. They sat on the couch. The TV got turned on. Not that they would watch it. More for some sort of noise to fill the space. It was quiet without Mitchell running around screaming his head off. Annie and David told him to keep quiet every time he did. Now wishing they hadn't. Just let the kid be a kid. It was a confusing time. Should they tell their extended families? It was a good idea, but it would have to wait a little while. They needed to get their bearings. Annie and David sat there. Not speaking. Waiting for the update the Uniformed Police Officer said they would give. Still holding hands from the police station.

They weren't letting go.

Not anytime soon.

Rita Allen

Natalie reminds me. I have some things to follow-up. She drives, I talk to Roger. I give them a call. On the fourth ring, the phone answers.

- Rita?

- How'd you know that?

- Tell your boss to give us a hurry up did you? If not you maybe Natalie?

- I haven't spoken with him since this morning. I don't think Natalie has either.

- Well, he's been on our case. We need answers. We need to know if there is a link. Who is the body? Where? What? How? And all those other questions bosses ask when they need the answer five days ago.

- Do you have any answers for those questions?

- A couple.

I look at Natalie, point at my phone, raise my eye-brows and nod my head to signal a positive direction.

Finally some answers.

- Still not able to identify the victim but their DNA was found at the scene of another incident involving a child. From some twenty years ago.

- Are you saying the body and the disappearance of Mitchell Winters are linked?

- This morning, the CD/DVD burn marks on the body and DVD found where Mitchell went missing could be written off as coincidence. This DNA evidence challenges that notion. We'd be silly now not too treat these two cases and separate incidents. In short, yes, they are linked.

- Anything else?

- The instrument used to cause the injuries to the victim's head
was most likely a crowbar. Or some other thin, solid metal object.
Metal fragments were found embedded in the victim's skull. That's a
first for me. We usually find that type of evidence in a stabbing or
car accident. Finding the fragments where we did indicates a very
severe impact to the skull. Brutal is the word which comes to mind.
Any closer to finding out where the victim may have been
murdered?

- Not as yet. On our way to another suspect now.

- Find me a murder scene. Other evidence. A name to follow-up.
As of now, we've exhausted all we can with the body from this
morning.

- What is the other incident?

- Other incident?

- The one involving the child you just mentioned.

- Ah, sorry, the child was never found. Went missing from the
front of a TV station. Twenty years was a while ago. I was just a
junior forensic. If I remember, the mother of the child was taking
him to an audition for a kids TV show. Afterwards, while waiting
for a bus or taxi, the mother was speaking to some other parents and
the child just disappeared.

- A TV station? Remember what one?

- Actually, now you say, the one in the footage from the DVD.
Let me look into some things. I think the mother may have had a
drug problem so there was some trepidation from investigators
about the veracity of the mother's claims. None of the other parents

remember seeing her with a child.

- But blood was found at the scene?

- Yes, that's all. Some blood on a hand rail leading up to the front door of the station. No-one could quite figure out where the blood came from. Or how it got there.

- Go look into that stuff and let me know.

The call ends. Brutal. Metal fragments in the skull. Whoever killed the victim must be harbouring a type of vengeance usually only found in horror stories. Who was the victim to their killer?

- Cases are linked, I tell Natalie.

- How?

- The DNA of the victim was found where a child went missing twenty years ago. Guess where the child went missing.

Natalie looks at me - Where?

- At the front of a TV station shown on the DVD.

She frowns.

I look out the car window. Maybe there are other missing child cases which could be linked to the body from this morning.

Then another thought hits me.

Maybe there are other unsolved murder cases which could be linked to the body from this morning.

I really don't like the direction this is going.

Ebony Bowen

We get to the shopping centre carpark. I see a few other news vans. They are here for the same reason I am. All are trying to get that single bit of information that separates their story from the others. We'll talk and see what each other has but hold some back in case the other person is unaware. No need to give a competitor a leg up, they need to climb on their own. There is some crime scene tape surrounding a space. A lone police person stands on watch. Inside the crime scene tape there are two people in protective clothing. Dusting the nearby bin for finger prints. Taking photographs of potential evidence. Getting data to create information to use to gain knowledge.

The wisdom will come when the crime is solved.

- See anyone you know?, asks Cary.

- I know most the other TV people. I know who they are but a couple from the newspapers and radio I've not met before. Media people are like a Venn diagrams, but with none of the circles overlapping or linking together.

- Tell me about it. You won't see the people who work camera's networking with the newspaper people. It's hard to put a visual video clip into a static bit of paper.

I start to mention that both of those media types have webpages where they probably put up video clips, then I think better of it and don't.

Cary finds a park near to where we need to be but far enough away to keep to ourselves.

Then he asks - What's the plan here? Just walk over and see if we can get some vox-pops from a witness or two? Speak to the security guard? Ask a police officer for what information they have?

All good questions.

- I'm not sure just yet. Let's get the camera setup and the sound recording mixed. By the time that's over, hopefully, by then we know what we're doing.

We get out the van and setup. Cary puts the camera on the stand and works the focus out. I stick a wireless microphone to the lapel of my jacket. I also get out a hand held mic so we can record people answering my questions. I can hear some of the other journalists.

- Did you see anything?

- Where were you when the parents realised their child was missing?

- What did you do when the parents realised their child was missing?

Standard questions. They need to be asked.

We all know what questions need to be asked. Why aren't the police kicking down the doors of every criminal they know? Why aren't politicians rushing in laws to build new prisons so the people who do these crimes can be put there forever? And those which affect me, why don't the media disclose their sources so the police can investigate fully? Why do the media focus on the populist or sensationalist aspects of crimes like this for the sake of ratings?

Important questions. They should be asked.

Its shouldn't need to be said why those things don't happen. Concerns for ethics. Social, perhaps legal, processes. Politics. We need to hold ourselves to a higher standard than criminals or we're just as bad as them. But you try telling a family of a victim of crime why kicking down a door of a known criminal is not the right way to go about it. Try explaining the ethics of journalism to parents looking for their missing child. Try explaining we need to do this right or some dodgy defence lawyer will exploit it for their own gain.

We walk over to where the parents were when Mitchell went missing. It feels empty. It's like not only a child went missing but so did any kind of energy that is associated with the shopping centre. I look at the car park and notice that it's only partially filled. I didn't notice that when we drove in but who actually checks how many vehicles are in a shopping centre carpark? It's not until you drive around looking for a park that you consider whether a carpark is full or empty.

I ask a security guard - Is the carpark usually this empty?

The security guard responds - No, had a lot more cars this morning but after what happened most people just left. Most of those cars are for the people who are working in the shops. Not many of them would be for customers.

I nod and walk away. We have to speak to the people who work here. Not the people who may or may not have been here this morning. People are prone to saying they were at an event when it happened. Any kind of scratching the surface soon shows the people were quite far away when the event happened. In that case, all you have is a narcissist making up answers to questions they have no business answering.

We've all been caught once or twice by that.

I mention to Cary - We need to speak with the people who work in the shopping centre.

Cary stops. Thinks. Nods. - Good idea, he says - anyone who was here this morning for their weekly grocery shop is long gone. Security probably changed shift over, or at least the guard who was here is with the police helping with their enquiries. We need to speak to the staff of the shops. Speak to someone from a phone store. Or the pharmacy or something.

We go inside the shopping centre. It's as empty as the carpark. There are some people are waking around. Mainly pensioners. Some of them are pushing a trolley while riding a mobility scooter. One or two sit on the benches provided wasting a minute before heading back to their homes. I cannot see any young couples. Or teenagers. Or families. The only young people I see are the ones working. I walk to the nearest shop which is an outlet for a mobile phone dealer. They see me walking towards them and after making eye contact with me they immediately look away. I'm not here to buy a phone and they're not here to answer any question that isn't about a phone.

- Hi, I'm Ebony Bowen from Channel 4 News, did you see anything this morning regarding the disappearance of a child?

They have a name tag. It says Yensharu.

- I didn't see anything. I was already in here when the police showed up, says Yensharu.

Yensharu isn't going to be much help.

- Thanks, I say and walk away.

I see another person in the kiosk directly across from the phone shop. It's one of those which sell the phone covers and do broken screen repairs. They are always outside the phone shops. They are never in front of clothing shops. I can see how they are watching myself and Cary. You can in it in people's eyes. When they have something they want to say. It's almost pleading, begging; please ask me, I have something to say. A good journalist recognises that look and uses it to their advantage. That look in their eyes, it's never something to look down on, regardless of how desperate it might seem. I walk over there.

Before I even get to the kiosk the person, Chen-Li but all her friends call her Chen I'm soon to be told, sticks out their hand to shake mine and says - Hi, I'm Chen-Li but all my friends call me Chen.

I shake her hand - Hi, I'm Ebony…, I start to say before getting cut off.

- Ebony Bowen, I know who you are. I'm studying journalism at uni. Are you here about this morning?

- Yes, I say - you have information?

- Nothing I haven't already told the police.

- And what was that.

- Am I allowed to tell you? The police wont arrest me or anything?

- We can blur your face, distort your voice and use a fake name if that helps alleviate your concerns.

- I don't know. I took a class last year about journalist ethics. I'm not sure I should answer. It might affect the police investigation. If it was only some vandalism maybe, but this is about a missing child.

- What did the police tell you when you told them?, says Cary.

Chen hesitates to answer.

- It's OK. He's with me, I say.

- The police said that if I remember any specific details to let them know.

I say to Chen - I think it'll be ok. You don't have any talk about any specific details. Just a broad overview of what happened. How about we get the camera going and I ask some questions?

- OK, says Chen.

Cary gets the camera setup. Holds out a bit of white paper to balance the lens. Checks the sound levels are good. Looks at me and goes - We're all good.

I ask Chen - What did you see this morning?

Chen begins - I was walking into work. The parents were looking into the jewellery store and I walked right behind them. I can't remember seeing the boy. I made it to the doors of the shopping centre then I heard the parents screaming. I didn't know what they were screaming about. Initially I thought he proposed to her and the screams were of joy. After a second I heard the fear in the screams. Then they were calling out, Michelle or Mitchell or some name like that. It was heartbreaking listening to them. I can't imagine what they are going through.

- Did the police tell you anything?

- No, just to call them if I remember anything.

- Thanks Chen, I say - you've been very helpful.

Chen says - I got to get back to work. Sorry I couldn't be more helpful.

We walk away. After a few steps I ask Cary - Does anyone ever see anything?

- I didn't see or hear a thing, says Cary.

Cary the smart arse. I look around. This place is not where I'm going to get the answers I need.

I say to Cary - Let's go, we need to look elsewhere.

Cary does not argue. He packs up the camera and we walk back out to the van. On the way out some of the other journalists look at us. There are mutual nods of the head in acknowledgement. None of us are giving out clues to our stories. We pack our gear in the van and start driving out. We're back at square one. Which as far as squares go, is probably the worse because it means we aren't moving forward.

A good journalist keeps up with the twists and turns.

Natalie Fenix

I know what I have to do. I'm just not sure how to do it. Matthew gave me a lead but it takes no psychic ability what so ever that I will need to speak to him again. He knows something. That he isn't forthcoming with it raises suspicions that it is important. But it will have to wait for a moment.

The person Matthew is suggesting I speak to is known as Chad. Chad isn't his real name. For the sake of legality, let's just leave his real name out of this. There are other people, good people, who share their name with Chad's real name. There is no need to get those good people caught up in this mess. Chad got stuck with that alias during one of his many court appearances. In one of them, it was found that he made the kids call him Chad for some reason. He wouldn't say why. When the court tried to find out why, Chad gave a small clue and the defence lawyer quit on the spot. When the court tried to appoint another lawyer, by then word had got around, no-one would represent him in court. It was then Chad saw the writing on the wall and, on the stern advice of the sitting judge, started taking plea deals. My colleagues call him vile, disgusting, perverted and, in some instances, a sick self-absorbed narcissist. Based on those court proceedings and from what I've read in police reports; those words are deserved. How do you approach a person like that? Unfortunate truth is, due to the plea deals, Chad has only been found guilty of minor offences resulting in short jail stints. Much to mine and my colleagues disappointment no-one has been able to make a more serious offence stick. If you grow up in the system you learn how to game the system to your own advantage. And it gets gamed. I've had the displeasure of meeting Chad a few times. I know where he is. I think the best approach is to knock on his door. Wait for the door to answer and then figure it out as it goes.

As we're driving I think about calling my husband. I decide not to. I hear the radio. I hear the news report. Kid. Police. Parents. Information. Help. It fades in. It fades out. I hear the advertisements. I hear the announcers. I hear the music. Darkness is not a light only medium. Darkness lives wherever it can. It feeds on culture, life, love; anything with energy. It is a parasite. I can hear the darkness in the sound. Everything is in a minor key. Voices. Music. Silence. Colour. Noise. Movement.

All of it.

We drive by the house we need to go to. There is no car. Windows closed. Tree's looking uncared for. Grass overgrown. It's no different to the other houses on the street. This area all but synonymous with unemployment. Crime. Violence. Lack of opportunity. Lack of upward mobility. Lack of a way out. An open air prison.

We drive around the corner and park the car. I take a few deep breathes. Rita does as well. Her's are deeper but with more soul. Mine just try to keep my head above water. We get out the car, walk to the house and walk up the driveway.

This is something that needs to get done.

I don't see any curtains move. Which is a good sign. Either we're not expected or we haven't been noticed. Then again maybe we are expected and some kind of bullshit is waiting for us as soon as we knock on the door.

I get to the door.

Knock knock.

I hear something bang, like a pot falling on the floor. Silence. I knock again and I hear the floorboards creak as someone walks to the door.

- Who is it?, goes Chad.

- You know who, I'm sure your pal Matthew Trenton has already told you I'd be here, I say.

- Yes, he did, and I'll tell you what I told him, says Chad.

- Yeah? What's that?, says Rita.

- Fuck off, goes Chad. Then he lets out this maniacal laugh.

This is going nowhere.

- I'm not doing that Chad, open the door. We need to speak, I say.

- What do I get out of it? A get out of jail card or something? says Chad.

- You get a free dental appointment to get your teeth straightened. Which is what you are going to need after I knock them crooked if you don't open this door, I say.

- And then I'm going to make sure a plastic surgeon won't be able to help, says Rita.

- Alright, hang on a second, says Chad.

We take a step back. Rita reaches for her gun. I do with mine. Chances do not get taken with people like this. The latch unlocks and we see the door go slightly ajar. I kick my leg right through the door. The door hits Chad right in his face. He goes flying backwards and falls over. I run into the hallway and as Chad is getting up I kick him in the face. He puts his hands up surrendering. Rita keeps her gun aimed at him. There is blood dribbling from his nose. The house smells like shit. As if sewerage has bubbled up from a drain. Not just one drain, all of them.

The smell is putrid.

I almost throw up.

- Calm down, fuck, stop, pleads Chad.

- Why do you think we're here?, I ask.

- I suppose you have a question you want answered, goes Chad

- A question?, says Rita.

- Fine; questions then, Chad spits.

He starts crawling backwards on the ground. I keep close, ready for a knife to be pulled out from somewhere. Getting stabbed in the leg. I'm ready for it. It looks like Chad has pissed himself. If he has I can't smell it. The smell of sewerage is overpowering. It's disgusting. The walls are smeared with something. Could be mud. Could be shit.

It's disgusting.

- The kitchen, can we go there? I need a paper towel. A glass of water maybe, goes Chad.

- Alright, the kitchen. You try anything and I will make sure you'll need more than a dental appointment and plastic surgeon, says Rita.

Chad picks himself up and goes to the kitchen. We follow him. When we get there I see a pot on the floor. The kitchen table is covered in what looks like bird shit. The sink is piled up with dirty dishes. Some cupboard doors are open. The shelves are lined with newspaper but the newspaper is covered in rat or mouse shit. Maybe even cat shit. Maybe, fuck, even human shit. The curtains have been drawn closed. I can't see the backyard. If I could, I'm sure the grass would be overgrown and rubbish would be everywhere. I don't think Chad is a hoarder, but the lack of cleanliness is disturbing. It puts the court proceedings and police reports in a new light. No wait, there is no light here. A new darkness. Light is going nowhere near this place.

- Cooking something?, I ask.

- Yes, soup if you were wondering, says Chad.

- We weren't, Rita replies without missing a beat.

- Trenchie give you my address?, Chad asks.

- Matthew Trenton, I say trying to keep some formality.

Chad stares at me.

- Trenchie or fuck off, he says with a hint of defiance.

- No, do you think a person like you isn't being watched by us? He just suggested we speak to you, Rita replies.

Chad sighs. You can tell he thought Matthew would have left him out of it. I don't know what went on with them two but one of them going to prison and the other not surely would have fucked with both their minds.

- So how'd you know I live here?, asks Chad.

- I just told you we keep tabs on you. Besides, don't you have to tell your parole officer when you move house or leave the state? Wouldn't information like that be added to a database we are capable of accessing when we need to?, says Rita.

- Well yeah, but I thought you'd get that information only if I did something wrong, Chad thinks out loud.

Neither Rita nor myself react. Narcissists always think they are the smartest person in the room. If they don't know something, then anyone who offers an answer is wrong.

- We can get that information whenever we want, I say.

I get the picture of Mitchell out my pocket. I don't look at it. I have a feeling that memory will rise. I'm not sure how I'll react if it does. I keep the picture facing Chad.

I ask him - Look at this picture, you know anything?

Chad takes the picture from me and looks at it.

This smell is disgusting. Like a public toilet that hasn't been cleaned or flushed for years, perhaps decades. I want to ask Chad, but I don't. I keep him focused on why we're here.

Don't allow an opportunity for a change in topic.

- Something about a missing kid was on the newsbreak a moment ago. Parents and all. Mommy crying. Daddy holding it together. You can tell he can't, gloats Chad.

- I can't hear a radio or see a TV on Chad, so how'd you know it was in a newsbreak?, I ask.

The smartarse pulls a mobile phone out his pocket and shows news webpage that's on it. The screen is cracked.

- Fuckhead's, you done that when you knocked me over kicking the door in.

- You know anything then?, Rita asks.

- Yeah, I guess the kid in the photo you got is the same missing kid mentioned in the newsbreak. People who take kids have no fucking care in the world about what some fucking parents think or their feelings.

It's a reasonable point. But it's clear Chad doesn't know the reason behind doing that. Police reports as shown on that newsbreak are aimed at people who might know who took the kid. Showing the parents in distress might make them feel guilty and give up some information to the police.

Chad will not get that information.

- Do you know who might have the kid now? Is he alive?, asks Rita.

- I'm sure the kid is still alive and I don't know who has him or where he is, replies Chad.

- What makes you think the kid is still alive?, I ask Chad.

- Fun. Whoever has him needs his fun first. Then the kid might be killed.

His response is unnerving.

- His?, I ask.

- Figure of speech. Correction your honour: They're, says Chad, thinking he is a step ahead.

But the Freudian slip is raising the hairs on the back of my neck. It's a he who done this. Not a she. Not a they. A he. There will be people who will say it is always a he then unleash a barrage of meaningless stats. Those people know shit. Stats can prove anything you want. She's and they's in this line of work are as fucked up as each other.

Good police look past stereotypes and stats to find a criminal.

- So who has him?, asks Rita.

- I don't know. Probably operates on his own time. In his own world. Scary fucker.

Chad keeps looking at the kid. I remember who I'm talking too. I grab the picture from him and put the picture back in my pocket.

- So where might this particular person be?, asks Rita.

- I really don't know, Chad says in a way that feels like the truth.

- I really think you do, I say.

- Well, I have heard of this house. Supposedly setup like the matador's maze. A house inside a house inside a house kind of thing, goes Chad.

- A house inside a house?, asks Rita.

- That's what I heard, goes Chad

- From who?, I ask knowing full well what Chad just did.

Chad frowns. He messed up here. Trying to keep himself out of shit but inadvertently put someone else in it. He knows he has to give me a name now.

- Err, stumbles Chad.

- Don't. Just don't. Who?, demands Rita.

- If I give you a name you can't say you got it from me. This person has a type of power that comes with wealth and knowing other people with even more wealth. That's no overstatement either, goes Chad.

- Okay. No promises. But okay, says Rita.

- Clarkson Glennis, says Chad in a way that makes him think we know exactly who he is talking about.

We do.

- What, the media-mogul?, questions Rita.

- The one and only, Chad says in a game show host voice.

- And who is he in all of this?, I ask.

- He is the door to the inner circle, Chads responds.

- Inner circle? You mean the mythological group called the Circles? The group the media love to mention in any unsolved crime that involves a missing child? The group every detective dreams of uncovering? The group of people made up of high level bureaucrats, old money types and other assorted taste and trend makers? Who is on the other side of the door?, I ask further.

- Don't know. Can't get by the door, says Chad.

He's checked out here. We have to finish this before he stops answering. Why is he giving this up? The next step in some plan? Narcissistic tendency to save himself?

I hear a child's voice in my mind say 'Be careful' and it frightens me. I can't show that now.

- What are The Circles?, I ask.

- Depending on who you are you get put in a circle. Me and Trenchie, we are on the outer circles. We both used to be further in but then you did what you did so I went one back and Trenchie got put out fully.

- He says he is done with it, states Rita.

- Yeah, like fuck he is. Him telling you lot to come speak to me is his effort to move inwards in the circles.

- Clarkson Glennis right?, I ask.

Chad goes - Media extraordinaire himself.

Rita shoots me a look like we're done here for now.

I agree. We're not getting any further useful information from Chad.

We walk out his house. He yells something but neither of us are interested. We're walking out to the car. When we get in the car I take a deep breath and start punching the air. I want to give up. The darkness sees this and grins. Goading me to do something not in my best interest.

Rita goes - You okay?

I say - Yep.

- You know what TV Station Clarkson Glennis worked for don't you.

I look at her. I want to say no. But it's a stupid response. - The one in the DVD footage from this morning, I say.

- Yep. That one. You know those burn marks on the body from this morning?

- Yeah.

- Circles, says Rita, she hands me her phone. On it is a picture of the burn marks. It's a circle inside a circle. - Want to hear something else?, asks Rita.

- No, I don't.

- I bet that if we were to find the object that caused those burn marks, and it will be a DVD, that they are the same brand as the one found from where Mitchell went missing, Rita prophesises.

Darkness laughs. It's a setup and we've walked straight into it. It's moments like this which proves the folly of fate. People don't win the lotto because of fate without the equal opposite event also happening somewhere else in the world.

- Find the kid, find the murderer, says Rita.

- Find what else?, I reply.

Rita starts the car and accelerates away. The tyres screech.

Clarkson Glennis. We go to his humble abode. Which is anything but. Lavish. Indulgent. Excessive. One of those houses you'd love to live in but because you don't; you'd love to trash instead.

I need to get this done.

Chapter 5

The other day I saw a cat pretending to be a giraffe. It was a surreal experience. No, it was a real experience. I think. Or it was another type of experience. Either way, I saw a cat pretending to be a giraffe. There was nothing surreal about it. Or real. Or something else. It seemed the cat was having an existential crisis. I asked the cat what its problem was but it pretended not to understand what I was saying and ran off.

My friend says something about not caring about a cat and giraffes are stupid and they just want to go home. I don't even know what surreal means.

I tell him to show some manners and be polite. I tell him most people don't know what surreal is.

Or I don't say that to him and I say something else completely.

He puts his hands over his eyes and doesn't say anything.

I tell him to stop playing games.

He doesn't respond.

I tell him if I have to get the crowbar out again it won't be good.

He takes his away from his eyes and shakes his head no.

I say good.

I ask him where do you think the cat ran away too?

He shakes his head no again and says I don't know.

I say to the other side of the road.

He screws his face up looking confused. Didn't the chicken cross the road he says?

I say sure, but I'm not talking about a chicken I'm talking about a cat.

Or I'm pretty sure I'm talking about a cat. I could be talking about a chicken. I can't tell anymore. I look at the crowbar. It can wait.

I ask him am I talking about a cat or a chicken?

He puts his hand over his eyes again and says I don't know. Then he starts crying.

This is really starting to fuck me off. I walk over to crowbar and pick it up. I start tapping on the door.

Do you want me to hit the door loudly again? You better start acting properly. Or I will start hitting the door. Worse than last time.
He takes his hands away from his eyes and wipes away his tears. He

says I really just want to see mom and dad. I don't want to play anymore. Let me go please.

I say soon. Maybe. If you're good. For now, let me know if I was talking about a cat or chicken. Or if I was talking about something else.

You were talking about a stupid cat and an even more stupid giraffe. But cats can't talk so why did you think a cat was talking to you?

Well, it wasn't talking to me I say.

So what was the cat doing?

For fucks sake, it was pretending to be a giraffe.

What does existence crisis mean?

It's existential and it means something. Or it means something else. But I don't know what else it could mean.

There is a knock on the front door. Or it sounds like a knock on the front door.

I ask my friend if he can hear a knocking on the door.

He nods his head.

I say are you sure?

He nods his head again.

I tell my friend not to go anywhere. Which he won't because he is locked up in a smaller room. I tell him to be quiet. But that doesn't matter because no-one is going to be able to hear him if he did make a sound.

I get up and go see who is knocking on the door.

Rita Allen

We're driving to the house of Clarkson Glennis. Find the kid, find the murderer. But Natalie did point out something. Find what else? I grab my phone out, hand it to Natalie to speak hands free. The call answers.

- Forensics. Roger Nelson.

- Rita here. Those burn marks on the victim this morning. Could they be from a DVD?

- Yes. You found one? It might not be out of shape, but it would have definite visible charring or heat strain.

- What about that missing child from twenty years ago?

- Yes, I looked further into that. Not much to add sorry. Child went missing. Name of Jayden Robins. Blood found at scene, which as I said earlier, is a match for the victim this morning. Lots of leads which led nowhere.

- What about the child's parent's? Who are they?

- Just a mother on the police report. Father known, but not around. Mother said he took off one day. Left her holding the child. She, an unemployed single mother at the time. But once the child went missing, fell into drug abuse. Homelessness. Then an early death. Most likely brought on by using drugs and homelessness.

- Got a mother's name?

- Report says Margaret Robins.

- Did this Jayden enrol at a school or kindergarten?

- No, we have nothing. Just a birth certificate. There are no immunisation details. No hospital reports. No school enrolments. No child care. It's possible a local GP has some paper records tucked away in a dusty box. It's possible there were records and have since been destroyed. Apart from the birth certificate. We have nothing.

- How could the police find a missing child when all they had is a name?

- I'm sure they tried. But as you know, new cases start and old cases with no new evidence get put into a box. Look, we're all done here with the body this morning. No more tests to run. Unless you get further evidence we are moving on. Other evidence from other crimes needs analysing.

- Ok, I understand. If we have anything, we'll get it to you, I say and hang up.

Natalie hands the phone back and I put it in my pocket.

We continue to drive, albeit in silence.

Natalie looks like she has the weight of the world on her shoulders. I wish she would open up sometimes. But I understand why she doesn't. No-one asks for what they get in life. Especially the bad stuff. She's on a mission, I guess she's well aware the mission might not be a success.

I think out loud.

- Jayden Robins.

- Who?, says Natalie getting drawn back to the here and now from wherever she was.

- The name of the kid who went missing in front on the TV station. Jayden Robins.

- What about him?

- There's nothing about him but a birth certificate.

- Where you going with this?

- Reminds me of those people who commit fraud. They go to a cemetery. Scan the names. Go online. See if they can change a detail or two. Get a new identity.

- Are you saying this Jayden Robins is just a red-herring? A new identity for someone else? Was the mother in on it as well? Perhaps the mother was associated with some shady characters that used her to get a new identity. Faked a child going missing?

- I don't know.

Natalie turns to look out the window.

We're getting closer to the house Clarkson Glennis. As you change from a poor suburb to an affluent suburb, the architecture of the house's change. The trees change from being poorly kept, low maintenance types to pruned hedges with immaculate lawn. The cars change from second-hand cheap imports to brand new luxury imports. The clothes change from the discount rack to the new season rack.

I've spoken to my husband about this. He is a little more blunt about it all. He says the difference between a poor suburb and a rich suburb is the poor people have no choice in the matter the rich people are born into it.

I don't disagree.

I'm about to say that to Natalie but we get to the driveway of Clarkson Glennis. We stop at the gate. They are huge iron ominous things. The shadow of the gates goes across the windshield. It looks like we're in a prison.

There is a sign on the front: 'Gates close at 6pm - Automatically'
We drive in.

I look in the rear view to see if there is anything written on the other side of the sign.

There isn't.

Natalie Fenix

We walk into the front office of the humble abode of Clarkson Glennis. It is gross just how over the top it is. There is a feeling of darkness. The light from outside seeps through the windows but the darkness holds steady in the area's the light doesn't shine on. We get to the front door.

Knock knock.

A person, who is not Clarkson Glennis by the looks of it, answers the door. A house maid or personal assistant or cleaner or something.

The Assistant tells us - He is not here at the moment and if we want to speak with him we will need an appointment.

- When can we get an appointment?, I ask.

The Assistant advises - Mr Glennis does not have any free time until next week.

That isn't going to cut it.

The Assistant apologises, saying - There is not much I can do about it. Priorities are priorities and time is a limited resource. Of which the Mr Glennis has little to spare.

I tell the Assistant - Call up Mr Glennis and say there are people here who would like to speak about the Circles.

The personal assistant says - The Circles?, in a way that suggests it's a question.

I say - Yes.

Although Rita is not wearing a watch, she taps on her wrist where a watch would be indicating time is ticking.

The Assistant calls Mr Glennis. Mentions the Circles. Says will do. Then hangs up the phone and goes - Mr Glennis will see you now. Please come in.

I say – Thanks, and we are directed to an office.

When we enter office he sees us and waves then holds up a finger that says just a minute please. I nod.

Looking around his office. There is a lot of money in here. I'm sure some of it is tax payer's money but some of it suggests old money. The mahogany table. Leather chairs. Bookcase full of legislation, bibles and a few history books. There are photos on the wall of him with a reverend or a famous sports star or celebrity of some kind. Some are of, what is most likely, his family. There is one on a wall but it is the only photo on the wall. It's him with someone else familiar but I can't place who.

Clarkson wears a well-tailored blue suit with a light blue shirt. The tie is a darkish red with black dots and brown shoes. Hair is well manicured and I'm pretty sure his face is covered with some blush. Either had a TV spot or is going to one.

He hangs up the phone and says - Sorry about that, he walks from behind is desk over to me and hold out his hand - I'm Clarkson Glennis. Please call me Clarkson.

We shake his hand and I tell him - I'm Detective Natalie Fenix and this is Detective Rita Allen.

He says - You're here about the Circles?

- Yes.

- I'm not sure what you mean.

- A source has given us your name in connection with the Circles.

- A source? What does that mean?

I remain silent. Rita gives him a deadpan look. We may have been a bit too quick to jump on someone's throat. We should have lead up to this but we don't have time. A child is missing. We need to get it done.

Then Clarkson says - I think there might be a misunderstanding here. The Circles, I'm not sure how I could be of any help.

Rita says - Is that why you decided to take this meeting with us? If you really didn't know anything you would've told your personal assistant out there to brush us off with some cliqued excuse like you have an important meeting with an even more important person.

- I do have an important meeting, replies Clarkson.

Rita responds - But not with an important person, so can we please get to where this conversation is heading quickly. The circles, what do you know?

Clarkson claims - I have heard of them. Only through secondary sources however. Gossip at a dinner party type thing. Some weird mix of people, supposedly who, are from the more upper echelons of society and they enjoy the company of children.

- Enjoy their company?, I ask.

- I don't know how to put it in a more interesting way.

I point to the single photo on the wall, - Who is that you're with?

Clarkson smiles -That was the arch-bishop who was potentially going to be a pope.

- So why didn't he?, asks Rita.

- Politics of the church. Backroom favours. Nasty rumours. You know how it goes.

We don't say anything. Clarkson continues.

- He was arch-bishop of this state for 17 years. Served at the Vatican for 12 years before he became the arch-bishop. That was the day before his retirement. That is Grayson Bell. Arguably the most influential arch-bishop this state, even this country, has had or will have.

- These upper echelons of society types, they ever interact with lower echelons of society types?, I ask.

Clarkson nods - Hence the circles. I really don't know how I can be of help here. Yes, I've heard mention of the Circles. Who they are as individuals? I have no idea.

- Willing to speculate on who?, Rita says with some hope of an accurate answer.

- Absolutely not. That is a potentially very litigious act and I am not opening myself up to costly lawsuits based on hearsay and speculation. What department are you with again?

- We didn't say anything about a department, I say – A source mentioned your name regarding a current investigation. Here we are asking questions.

- I have no idea how my name was given to you. Who gave my name to you? I have a lawyer who loves sending cease and desists.

- We have to protect our sources like you protect your sources in the media when it comes to making the news, says Rita with dismay.

Clarkson is well aware of this.

- Yes, well there is a line in journalism which can be crossed. Particularly if it involves a criminal act against a child or another person. We are obligated to report it to the police, he says.

- Even then that depends on who the source is, I add.

- I really don't know what you are insinuating here. There is nothing I can say that will be helpful.

- What do you know that you're not telling us?, asks Rita.

Clarkson says - In this situation, nothing.

Rita further says - Seems you're in a no win situation. Tell, get sued for defamation. Don't tell. Get the wrath of the advertisers you work with.

- The media are like steroids, says Clarkson - Always making something artificially bigger. The moment it goes away everything goes back to normal. Besides, if I don't know anything I got nothing to worry about. What's that old saying? If you're innocent you can't be found guilty.

- You have no information regarding the Circles?, I ask as a final question.

Clarkson says with a note of superiority in his tone - I can't speak for that. Is there anything else?

- Do you have any information on the whereabouts of Mitchell Winters?, I ask.

- Mitchell Winters?, asks Clarkson.

- Yes, the young boy who went missing this morning, I say.

I hold the picture of Mitchell out so Clarkson can see. He leans in and looks at the picture. A look of recognition draws across his face. I put the picture back into my pocket.

- Oh yes, that young boy from the news reports. No, I don't know his current whereabouts. I'm sorry I have not been much help here. Any further questions?, Clarkson says looking first at me then at Rita.

- No, not at the moment. But if we have another question?, says Rita.

- Please contact my Assistant and we'll try our best to get the right answer.

I nod and we leave.

On our way out the Assistant asks - Is there is anything else we need?

I say - If we come by this office or make a phone call I don't want to wait.

The personal assistant says - The offer was only meant as an act of customer service.

I don't say anything. We leave the office. We step outside. Although the sun is shining away, the house casts a shadow as though it has a Narthex and Spires. The shadow hangs over Rita and myself.

Rita goes - I'm hungry.

Even though I'm not, I will eat.

I say - So could I.

Annie's phone rang. It was her sister Bekka. Younger by two years. Single. No kids. Loved Mitchell as much as Annie and David. Had recently met a guy who had been married before. Both him and his ex. lost their jobs about the same time and their marriage hit the wall. He saw the bottle. She saw the door. However, that was the past and he had moved on. Annie and David had both met him and he looked like he had changed direction with his life. They both worked in a factory. There was talk of marriage, kids and building a home. Time would tell that story. However, as cool as an aunt might be, no way were they going to love a kid as much as the kid's parents. Growing up Annie and Bekka had been inseparable. Not much had changed into their adulthood. Bekka was in tears but more concerned with how Annie was feeling.

Annie said - I'm holding up for the time being. Still in a bit of shock. Hasn't quite sunk in yet. Tomorrow morning would be where it hit. Unless Mitchell was found before then.

Annie, very hopeful he would, was trying her best to stay calm.

Bekka sensed this and asked - Should I come around?

Annie said - No.

Took a breath.

Annie said – Yes.

Then, more sure of her answer, Annie said - Yes.

Bekka, if she could have, would have clicked her fingers and been there in an instant. She lived half an hour away.

Bekka asked - Do you want me to tell Mum and Dad or do you want to?

Annie said - You do it.

Bekka said - I'll call, then be on my way.

Annie resigned herself to more waiting.

She told David - Bekka is on her way.

David didn't argue. He knew Annie's relationship with Bekka was strong. David didn't have a brother or sister. An only child. Both his parents had passed away within 6 months of each other a few years ago. They both got to meet Mitchell. He was glad he could share that with his parents. For David, his life was Annie and Mitchell. Then he remembered he had a job and he was certain his colleagues would read the paper or watch the TV. He wasn't calling them. Not now. Probably not tomorrow either. He didn't know when. When was a good time to tell your employer your child is missing? He would wait for them to call him. Annie's phone rang again. It was her Mum. Phone was on speaker. Dad was there too. Mum was hard to understand. Annie couldn't make much out of it. She understood why. Annie was surprised she wasn't sounding like that herself. Dad bought a measure of calm to the conversation. But only barely.

Annie said - Bekka is on her way.

Mum said - Yeah she just called. We would be as well but it's a day and a half drive. We wouldn't be leaving until tomorrow morning.

Dad said - I'm getting the car ready for the drive. We'll be there as soon as we can.

The call ended.

All Annie and David could do now was wait.

Wait for the police to find Mitchell.

Wait for Bekka to get here.

And wait for Annie's parents to get here.

Waiting sucked at the best of times.

When a missing child was involved, waiting seemed like a cruel joke.

Chapter 6

Before I hear the knock on the door I know it's going to be those two Circle conformist fucks.

Who are just two examples of Circle conformist fuck's.

There are many of them, some you may have heard of before. Them being part of that upper ruling class/public service class elite. I shouldn't be telling you any of this. I know the Circle's. I know who is in it. Well, mainly who is in those outer circles like these two Circle conformist fucks. I know a few of the inside Circler's. Some of them too well.

Some of them intimately, but it's been a while since that last happened.

But to hell with it. I'm done. Or I think I'm done. Maybe I'm something else.

Those Circle people, sure enough they have been on your TV screen. On your radio speaker; be it car speaker or headphones. And maybe your social media mediums of choice. But I don't know much about social media mediums except you may as well put a flashing sign above your head saying here I am, look, I'm right here. I am quite happy with people not knowing where I am. I am forever only ever going to be right here.

I know it's going to be those Circle conformist fucks because I got a visit from someone earlier, who I'm sure I'll need to see again later, who told me I've made something visible that should not. An attempt to show some muscle after the phone call I got. I was told to fix it. Some people are angry. Loose ends need to be tied up. Or cleaned up. One of them, I'm told to put them outside the circle. I'm told to put a line through their name. I don't know who they mean. They all talk so vaguely and they think somehow I know who they mean. Which I don't. Maybe I do. I don't know. It's possible they meant me but I didn't know it so they just told me to deal with it as if I knew who they meant. So I am going to assume they meant these two.

Or presume.

There is a knock. Then another. And another. Like some secret code except I don't know what the fuck they're on about. I answer the door and sure enough, Circle conformist one, a.k.a. Trenchie, is standing there. Standing next to him is the other fucking idiot we will call Circle conformist two, a.k.a. Chad. A good narrator would have introduced these two earlier in the story. Foreshadowing. Alluding. Red herrering-ing. But I'm not the narrator so I wouldn't know shit all about that.

I bet you're waiting for an "or".

I am going to dictate to you the dialogue I have with the two Circle conformist fucks after I opened the door. To do that, I will be referred to as Number 2 Male. Circle conformist fuck number one, a.k.a. Trenchie, will be Circle Conformist Fuck Number One. And, Circle conformist fuck number two, a.k.a. Chad, will be Circle Conformist Fuck Number Two.

I know this is getting confusing but that's the point. Do some research into linguistic deviancy in crime fiction. Read some Paul Auster. Go for a walk. Get a dog. Go to a new restaurant. Watch a Sophia Coppola movie. I know everything that was mentioned after Paul Auster has nothing to do with linguistic deviancy. Point is, do fucking anything instead of having a whinge about this story because in all serious dear reader, I don't give a fuck about you.

Or maybe I do and I'm just being antagonistic.

Anyway.

Number 2 Male starts with: What the fuck you two want?

Circle Conformist Fuck Number One replies with: We need to talk about something.

Number 2 Male goes: So what's the something then?

Circle Conformist Fuck Number One goes: Hold on, I'm getting to that.

Circle Conformist Fuck Number Two follows up saying: Patience. 'Cause what's coming your way if you don't fucking straighten your shit out ain't pretty.

Number 2 Male responds: What does straighten mean?

Circle Conformist Fuck Number Two does one of those confused faces looks and says: It means (then he pauses, he definitely doesn't know what it means), it means fall in line.

Number 2 Male asks: Is there an or else?

Circle Conformist Fuck Number One says: No.

Number 2 Male goes: Ok. Is that it?

Circle Conformist Fuck Number One says: No, we need to look through your house. We were told you were going to not do the thing you've already done.

It seems the person who saw me earlier to fix something has set these two up by saying the same thing to them and put me in the shit. Or in something else. Like a line. Which Circle Conformist Fuck Number Two knows absolutely nothing about.

Number 2 Male says: That's a confusing statement. Can you re-phrase into something a little more intelligible.

Circle Conformist Fuck Number One goes: No.

Number 2 Male says: Ok, so now what then?

Circle Conformist Fuck Number Two shakes his head like I'm being difficult and says: We look through your house you stupid fuck.

Number 2 Male says: You weren't nearly so tough a few years ago. Didn't you put your friend here in jail to keep yourself out?

Circle Conformist Fuck Number One looks at Circle Conformist Fuck Number Two waiting for an answer. Number 2 Male is also waiting for an answer. Circle Conformist Fuck Number One doesn't answer; just looks at the ground and with that Number 2 Male knows he just has to worry about Circle Conformist Fuck Number Two. It looks like Circle Conformist Fuck Number One knows this as well.

Circle Conformist Fuck Number One raises his voice and says: Let us in. Look around. See what's up. Then we can go if all looks good.

Pardon me for breaking into the narrative while I describe this dialogue but I need to do something here before these two imbaciles draw too much attention to this here situation. Which is; I need to make sure my new friend is doing okay. I haven't put another bottle of water or packet of chips into the room my friend is in.

Number 2 Male says: Ok, come in. Look around. Then leave.

Circle Conformist Fuck Number One goes: Sounds good.

This is where I am going to stop describing the dialogue. Circle Conformist Fuck Number One walks in first followed by Circle Conformist Fuck Number Two who is still looking at the ground. Once they are inside I get the baseball bat that was behind the front door and crack it into the back of Circle Conformist Fuck Number One's head. That useless fuck falls down quick. Because I forgot to close the door, well I didn't forget it was more strategical, had I closed the door they would have seen the baseball bat. Anyway, Circle Conformist Fuck Number Two runs out. I go to follow him out the door but think better of it. I watch Circle Conformist Fuck Number Two run towards a car. He gets in and tears away. I turn and go back inside. I close the door. I don't need anyone to see what I'm about to do.

Inside Circle Conformist Fuck Number One is lying on the ground. One of his hands is holding the back of head. It's covered in blood. Some of which as dripped onto the floor. Which I'm going to have to clean up later. He's moaning or saying some shit like don't or stop or some other word I haven't thought up yet. I smack the baseball bat down just below his knees. He curls up and grabs the back of his legs. Shouting something. I can't hear what. Not that I can hear anyway. I smack the baseball bat onto his legs below the knees again. He stays curled up. Still shouting. I smack him again this time above the knees. He takes it this time. Getting the picture. Screaming didn't stop this for him, perhaps silence does. I agree with his choice. To prove it I hit him again above the knees and yell in his face - Maybe you should've shut the fuck up to begin with and then maybe this wouldn't have happened. Hey?, Not that I'm asking a questions that needs an answer.

I give it a moment and I can hear his breathing slow down. I crouch down below and lean in close to his ears.

tick tock tick Tock tick TOck tick TOCk tick TOCK Tick TOCK TIck TOCK TICk TOCK TICK…

… and I say open your eyes…

He does.

I stretch back as far as I can and bring the baseball bat down across his face. Shit flies everywhere. It's most satisfying. On eye has disappeared. The other eye looks at me still in the part of the skull that hasn't been shattered. There is no light behind the eye. There was no light behind the eye beforehand.

I scream into his lifeless face.

I kneel down. In the puddle of pooling blood, I draw a circle. Then I draw a circle inside that circle. Then I draw a line right through the middle of both.

I stand up and throw the baseball bat on the ground then go into the kitchen. I get some hand towels and wipe whatever it is that has covered my face. I look at the towel. It is red. I look at my hands, they're red to. I look back at where Circle Conformist Fuck Number One is. The floor is covered in red. There is a bit of cleaning up to do. I have enough supplies to get this sorted. Will I have to go back to the shop to re-supply? This was an unexpected event. What the fuck were those two fucks thinking? When the person who saw me earlier saw them, they should have said no or just got out of town. Whatever, that's their problem now. Well, for one of them anyway. The other one doesn't have any more problems. Ever.

I know exactly what I'm going to do with the body of Circle Conformist Fuck Number One.

I'm actually kind of excited by the thought. I wish I thought of something like this sooner. Those Circle fucks and their stupid games.

Enough of the talk. I'm going to be a bit busy for the next hour or two. Before I do, I get some water and chips for my friend. I go into his room and put them next to his door. It looks like he is asleep. I'm not finding out if he is or isn't. I really don't need to deal with another person screaming. One is enough. I leave the room where my friend is in. Crowbar still leaning against the door. I move it to right in front of the cage he is in. So when we wakes up, that is the first thing he will see. I close the door. I walk to the lounge room at the front of my house and look out the window. It seems Circle Conformist Fuck Number Two has gone away for good. There are no neighbours peeping about. All good signs.

I get to work cleaning up this mess.

… TOCK.

Annie heard Bekka's car turn into the driveway. Usually she would be out of chair, through the front door and giving Bekka a hug before she even got out her car. Not today. Today Annie stayed on the couch. She wanted to do that but not while Mitchell wasn't here. As much as Mitchell hated kisses from his Mum he hated them from his Aunt Bekka even more. Mitchell mentioned more than once that it was gross. Annie and Bekka always laughed at that. David had heard Bekka car as well. He looked at Annie wondering if she was going to greet her sister. She stayed on the couch. David got up from his seat and opened the door just as Bekka was about to knock.

- Hey, said David.

- Hey, said Bekka.

They looked at each other. Nothing much more could be said. They hugged then David stepped aside and Bekka walked through the door. Annie looked up and saw Bekka smiled in relief. Just as quickly the smile came it went.

Annie got up off the couch to give Bekka a hug. They both broke down. David stood to the side. A tear welling up in his eyes. Annie saw him, reached out and brought him into the hug. The three of them stayed embraced for a minute or two then broke apart.

David says – I'll put the kettle on.

He didn't move and stood there trying to figure out what was supposed to happen after saying he'd put the kettle on. Bekka watched then traced David's line of sight to a picture of Mitchell on the bookshelf.

Bekka, taking control of the moment, said - I'll go put the kettle on. Walking to the kitchen Bekka yelled out - When was the last time you two ate?

- This morning, Annie replied with a hint of monotone in her voice.

Bekka got to the kitchen and saw the breakfast dishes drying in the rack next to the sink. Everything else looked untouched. There were no cups or partly empty water bottle out. No crumbs of food on the bench. It looked like when Annie and David got home they sat on the couch and haven't moved since.

- Coffee or tea, Bekka yelled out.

- Tea, David said back.

After asking the question Bekka thought coffee would be bad idea and then wondered why she asked a question that had an obvious answer. She filled the kettle and plugged it in. Got three cups out the cupboard. Put a teabag in each. She got a tray out another cupboard. On it she put a cup of sugar and a jug of milk. She had been here many a time and knew the layout of the kitchen well. She waited a few minutes. Listening to the sounds in the kitchen.

Initially, silence. Then s dog from a neighbour barked. A petrol powered machine started up. A whipper snipper or lawn mower or something. Then the dog barked louder for longer. The kettle boiled.

She tipped the hot water into another jug. Put that on the tray. Then took to the tray out to Annie and David. She knew their tea order. Annie took one sugar no milk. David had two sugars and milk. She made them their tea. Made herself one, sat on a nearby couch and sipped at her tea. Annie and David each sipped at theirs.

Bekka asked – Have the police given you an update or anything yet?

- No, said David - not yet. After the station they said to go home and if they get any information they will let us know.

- They haven't called with any new information yet, added Annie.

- Mum and Dad call?, asked Bekka.

Annie nodded - They are on their way and will be here about this time tomorrow.

Bekka sipped her tea again then asked - Do you want me to get some dinner? Even if it is just a slice of toast or sandwich?

Annie shook her head no - I'm really not hungry.

Annie sipped her tea. The warmth of the tea provided a momentary feeling of comfort. Then the reality of the situation came back. Annie wondered if this is what soldiers feel when they are at war and they think the fighting has stopped only for it to start back up again.

David said - Some food might be helpful. He looked at Annie. She caught his eye and had to agree food would be nice.

Bekka nodded - I'll find out if the restaurant down the road delivers.

- Nothing big, David stated, I'm with Annie in not feeling that hungry but half a sandwich is going to help.

Bekka got out her phone and started getting some food delivery organised. A few taps and touches. Some scrolling and a few more taps and touches. Some food was on its way.

- Be here in about thirty minutes said Bekka.

They waited the thirty minutes. Not much was said. In fact nothing was said. Bekka put the TV on to provide some sort of reference to work from. Annie looked like she was watching the TV but she seemed to be a million miles away. David sat rubbing his forehead. Deep in thought where the thought was also a million miles away. Most of the day had taken forever to get through but the thirty minute wait time for the food went by in moments. There was a knock on the door. Bekka got up, got the food and when back in the lounge room started unpacking. Some tubs of salad. A couple of sandwiches. Mini-packets of sauce and mayonnaise. Both Annie and David stepped back into the present.

- Thanks Bekka, said Annie and reached out for a sandwich. She took a few bites and put the sandwich back. It would remain there, without being touched further, for some time.

David did similar.

They watched the TV. Ate their food and let the time pass. It had to. Time was not going to do anything else. The news came on. Bekka got up to reach for the remote to change the channel but was stopped by Annie who said - Don't, leave it.

So they watched the news. Mitchell's story was second. First was some politician that said something ridiculous on a social media platform. The news finished. Bekka collected the leftover food and put it in the fridge. She noticed a card with a phone number for a detective. She stuck the card to the fridge with a magnet. The evening moved into the night. The news finished the movies started. Annie David fell asleep on the couch. Nearing midnight Bekka got up and went to a spare room.

Bekka left the TV on.

Natalie Fenix

Rita. She's talking out loud but to herself. Trying to figure out what food to eat. I don't have an opinion on what to eat. There is something else on my mind. I try my best to keep it suppressed. It's like walking a tightrope. A gentle sway either way and you fall off. When it happened initially my world fell apart. My partner's world just as fallen. We were devastated. It made me join the police. It made me become a detective. Although I have found many of the type of people I am looking for. I still haven't found the one I'm really after. The darkness still overpowering the light.

I can make out the shadows but nothing else identifiable. All I can see are invisible shadows. Every step I get closer they take a step further away. The invisible voices getting louder. As the darkness blocks the light; the voices block all the other sounds. A lone hand scribbles aimlessly on a wall indecipherable messages.

Then life makes itself known again.

Rita says - How 'bout Thai?

I say - That will work.

Rita says - Nah, we had that the other day. What's nearby?

I look around to see where we are - Seems like its Thai or fish 'n' chips.

- Fuck it, Thai it is, says Rita.

I don't question the decision. I think I'm leaning towards the braised cashews and vegetables with a can of cola.

- Braised cashews and vegetables for you?, asks Rita.

I look at her and smirk. We've been working together for too long – And a can of cola.

Rita goes - Well I'm going out on a limb and getting something

I've never had before.

Which I've heard many times before and many times it hasn't happened. I'm fairly certain Rita will order Pad Thai.

We get to the Thai shop and make our orders. Without skipping a beat Rita orders Pad Thai. I put mine in. Fifteen minutes later we're sitting on the table and chairs at the front of the shop. I grab a wooden bio-friendly fork. I take the lid off my food and pick at a few pieces of vegetables. The warmth of the food and the taste is comforting.

- Clarkson Glennis, I say or ask. More ask.

- Yeah, seems like there is a bit more going on behind the scenes, replies Rita.

- Everybody has heard the rumours about the Circles. Why would he play dumb and pretend he didn't know what we were talking about?, I question.

- It is a bit of a red flag. Makes me think there is something we should be getting told but aren't, says Rita.

- He won't tell us unless he really needs to. An ace up his sleeve. Will only get it out when absolutely required.

- So how do we get to that point?

And she raises a good question. How do you make someone do something when they don't want to or have no reason to?

- Should we go speak to Grayson Bell?, I ask.

- Yes. But I think we need to do that last. We need some sort of leverage that will convince both Grayson and Clarkson that the best thing to do is speak to us, Rita responds.

Which I didn't want to hear because it means we have to speak to Matthew Trenton and Chad again. I still can't get the smell of shit out of my nose since we visited Chad earlier.

What are we missing? Is there another direction or lead we can follow? Should we go back to the shops where Mitchell went missing? Have the media found something they aren't willing to share? All questions asked to Rita but none can really be given an answer.

- I think we would have had a call by now if the shops had any more information. I'm surprised at how little evidence or information is being found. Not a fingerprint. Not a hair. Not a witness. Are we chasing ghosts or something? If the media have found something they know better than to keep it from us. I think Matthew Trenton and Chad are our best option, states Rita.

Sounds like tomorrow's plan is sorted.

We're nearing the end of our meal. I've pretty much ate as much as I can. There are a few pieces of vegetables left in my tray but I'm done. It's this moment after dinner I dread most. The day is done. I have nothing else to do to keep my mind active. I could read a book or do a crossword puzzle but a distraction is just a moment. Soon enough the memories will start their mocking.

Start with their threats.

Their harassment.

They know they can hurt and they know how.

- Alright, I got to get home for a few hours, says Rita.

We get up, pay our bill and leave.

Neither of us say much on the brief drive. Both of us lost in thought. Trying to figure out if we've over-looked something. Forgot to ask someone a question that should have been asked. Missed a frame on the security camera footage. Misunderstood a comment made by someone.

Rita drops me off at the motel I'm staying. We say our see you later's and arrange for an eight in the morning pick-up time.

I've always stayed away from my family when I work. I don't need to be bringing work home. I can't talk about it if I wanted to. Your partner is there trying to connect but all you can do is put up a brick wall which just causes resentment. Resentment causes bitterness. Bitterness causes doubt and doubt is bad news. Better to stay away. A day is too long but an hour is even longer.

I look at the clock. 21:36.

I fall face down onto the bed. I close my eyes. I wait. I take a breath. Nothing happens. I roll onto my back and look at the ceiling. The ceiling goes out of focus and I start to look past the plainness of the white paint. It spins. I see a young face. Not Mitchell Winters. A memory of a face. I feel like I'm about to vomit. I push the memory down. Further. The feeling of needing to vomit subsides.

I take another breath.

I open my eyes.

I look at the clock. 04:42.

These next few hours are going to take forever.

Chapter 7

Circle Conformist Fuck Number One, a.k.a. Trenchie, would be easier to move if I had machines to do it for me. But I don't so the heavy lifting is wearing on my patience. If I had a body I would work out more which would make the heavy lifting easier. But I don't have a body so I don't work out

I have kicked Circle Conformist Fuck Number One, a.k.a. Trenchie, several times now and not once has there been a reaction. I probably should have cleaned up the mess, had a break and then sorted this out but life never works out the way you want. Even if you plan.

I manage to drag Circle Conformist Fuck Number One, a.k.a. Trenchie, to the back of my van. I open the back door. Some rubbish falls out. Paper. Rags. Empty cans of whatever product was in there before I drank it. Which was cola. Or orange juice. Or coffee. Or something else drinkable.

Head. Arms. Body. Legs. All things which I don't have make their way into the back of my van. Finally. I catch my breath. Pat my pockets. Van keys in the right trouser pocket. If I had a mobile phone, which I don't, it probably would have been in my left hand trouser pocket. I walk to the driver's side of the van, open the door, get in the van, start it up, get the garage door open and drive out. I stop just outside the garage and close the garage door. I don't leave until the door has fully closed. It shuts and I drive off.

To my destination.

To the abode of one of the main Circles.

One that I know about.

To working residence of Clarkson Glennis.

Yes, that Clarkson Glennis.

Don't try and pretend you haven't the rumours about this person. Not that I've seen any rumours with my own eyes. I don't have any. I don't think rumours are an actual physical object which can be seen. But that's beside the point. The point is the rumours are true. All of them. I know from experience. And our recently departed friend, Circle Conformist Fuck Number One, a.k.a. Trenchie if you forgot, would have agreed the rumours are true.

Driving through the suburbs. One place is the same as the next. The next follows and what follows is one place. And it just goes on and on. Same thing with shopping centres. Same thing with industrial centres. Same thing with the same things. It gets boring quick.

I get to the outskirts of the city. Nothing has changed except the same things are a little bigger. A little brighter. Costs a bit more money. I'm not going to talk about cars unless the narrator has other ideas.

Which they don't.

Here it is; the moment in time when it's time to act and your heart rate increases. My heart rate does not increase. I don't have a heart because I don't exist. That or I am what psychologists call "A Psychopath". But I can't be because I don't exist. Time seems to slow slightly. I turn the corner and the cathedral like place where I'm going occupies some of the space but comes across as though it occupies all the space. I look for camera's sticking out a wall. Or hanging off the corner of a building. It looks like they all seem to focus on the front of the building. The sides are out of focus. I know where Circle Conformist Fuck Number One, a.k.a. Trenchie, is going to end up. I turn into a road just before the main entrance of the Clarkson's house. I stop right out front. The cameras will see but are so far back from the roads the details won't be noticeable. I climb into the back of my van while inside the van. I don't get out. I push Circle Conformist Fuck Number One, a.k.a. Trenchie, up as close as I can to the back of the van. I unlatch the door. I push Circle Conformist Fuck Number One, a.k.a. Trenchie, out. His body pushes the van door ajar and eventually falls out the back. I pull on the frame of the door to get it partially closed. So I can drive off without the back door flying open as I drive away or turn a corner. My heart rate is slightly quicker. Or it hasn't changed rate at all. Which is more likely because I either don't exist or I am a psychopath. Increased heart rates do not happen in people like that. I drive straight. No U-turn. Straight ahead only.

When I get back to my house and get out my van I notice I didn't take the fake magnet business logo I have on the side. I pause and think of the ramifications of that. And after a beat I say fuck it out loud. Or I think it out loud. It's not like it's a registered business with an address to send mail to. Fake name. Fake phone number. Fake sign. Registration plates are real but I stole them off a similar van. I will need to get another set of registration plates.

I spend the rest of the night thinking about what will happen when Circle Conformist Fuck Number One, a.k.a. Trenchie, is found. I put the TV on but it is pointless. Just advertisements for a fancy kitchen utensil or fitness equipment. Or cleaning product. Or a handy tool to have around the house that has 73 different ways to be used where the ad goes through all 73 uses. Or something else people don't need but are somehow convinced to buy. Or something that hasn't even been invented yet. It gets boring quick. I turn off the TV. No light. No sound. For the first time in a long time I fall asleep in my chair.

I haven't even checked on my new friend since earlier.

Rita Allen

I get home hoping to see my kids before they go to sleep. Husband too.

But it's not the case. Kids have crashed out. Husband too.

I go the fridge, grab the half bottle of wine, a glass, grab my laptop, go to the couch, make myself comfortable and start going through some old case notes.

Namely, the missing child from the TV station.

I start reading. Kid reported missing by mother. Blood found at scene, which we now know matches with the victim from this morning. No-one witnesses remember seeing a kid.

Victim from this morning still unidentified.

It doesn't take long. My eyes get tired.

I look at a clock 22:56.

I fall asleep on the couch.

With the TV on.

DAY TWO

Natalie Fenix

04:43.

I sit up. I go to the bathroom. Splash some water on my face. Rinse my mouth out. Sit on the end of the bed. I reach into my overnight bag and get out my laptop. I wait for it to boot up. Thankfully no updates. I manoeuvre to the web browser and in the search bar I type: Grayson Bell. I don't know why I'm not searching for Clarkson Glennis. Something in the way Clarkson pointed out Grayson. There was an element of deference. Respect. Perhaps awe, in Clarkson's tone of voice. Now I think it over, it was unusual. It got my interest and the browser delivers its results.

A couple of social media accounts which look like they belong to other Grayson Bell's. I scroll down. None of the results seem relevant. I click to the next page of the search results. I scroll some more then there is a result. A news article written by an Ebony Bowen. It is from ten years ago. Title of the article is: Church Embroiled in further Child Abuse Claims. I click on the link. It takes me to a firewall. I type in my credentials and the article opens. I read it.

It's not enlightening. I remember these events. Some pastors doing some dodgy shit with kids. In a boys home. In a girls home. Mainly boys. Girls talk, boys don't. Not about stuff like that. Always after classes in an office or storeroom. Always when no-one else was around.

Like I said, dodgy shit.

I go back to the search results. I scroll through further. Click to the next page of search results. I scroll some more. I change up the search words. Scroll. Click. Scroll. Click. Some church based websites that mention Grayson Bell. I click the links. Nothing but pictures of church sermons. Community days. Conversations with other political or business leaders. Promotional propaganda which communicates nothing to see here. I do a search on Clarkson Glennis. There might be a similar story about the media being embroiled in child abuse claims. I doubt it though, the media is quite happy to throw stones but not at itself.

It's as though someone has done a data scrub on Clarkson. For someone who is so prominent and visible, there is a surprising lack of information about him online.

I look at the clock again. 04:57.

Fuck.

I stare at the screen. Figuring out what else to search. It feels like twenty minutes.

I look at the clock again. 04:59.

Fuck.

I go to my overnight bag and get some shorts and t-shirt. I start doing some stretches. Put my sneakers on. Do some more stretches. Grab the motel key. Head out and start running.

At first all I can hear is the sound of my feet hitting the concreate. The cadence becomes hypnotic.

Doof. Beat. Doof. Beat.

After a while I begin to hear my breathing.

In. Out. In. Out.

Doof. In. Beat. Out. Doof. In. Beat. Out.

Some cars drive by. Some trucks. Going to their jobs. Early starts for minimum wage. I begin to smell the city. The rubbish. The smoke. The factories. The pollution. It sounds the same as it smells. The smell of a rubbish truck collecting trash. The sound of a street sweeper vacuuming the gutter. The sound of the red-eye planes taking off. Engines a bit louder on a cooler morning. I keep running.

In. Beat. Out. Doof. In. Beat. Out. Doof.

Grayson Bell. Clarkson Glennis. The church. The media. I stop thinking about both and focus on the people who are part of both. It's the people who are the path to where I am going. I need to ask Clarkson Glennis about those nasty rumours. I need to find out if Grayson Bell still lives in the city. I need to speak to Matthew Trenton again. I will probably have to speak to Chad again.

Fuck. I keep running.

Beat. Out. Doof. In. Beat. Out. Doof. In.

I start circling back to my motel. The thoughts of who I need to speak to merge into one. The surface is jagged. Uneven. Sharp. Dangerous. Anything but plain. It provides a welcome change of context. There is a brief glimmer of a memory. Then it goes. Back to its waiting room. Ready to appear at the most inappropriate time. I'm sure the memory will kill me.

Nothing else has.

I keep running.

Out. Doof. In. Beat. Out. Doof. In. Beat.

I get back to my motel room. I catch my breath. I stretch to cool down. I go inside the motel room. I look at the clock.

06:19.

Good.

I put my phone on charge. I grab a shower. Dress. Put the little amount of make-up I usually use on. I check my gun. Get my badge.

Take my phone off charge. Then head to an early open café for breakfast. I remember running past one earlier. I go there. It's not far from the motel. Ten to fifteen minute walk. It is open. Bottle of water. Cup of coffee. Toast. I ask for the time.

06:59.

I call Rita. She has kids. They will be awake. As any parent knows. If your kids are awake; so are you.

Rita answers the phone - It's not even seven yet what do you want?

- We need to go back and talk to Clarkson, Matthew and Chad again. Probably even Grayson Bell. Something about him. One of those police hunches.

- Hunches? Why is it police have hunches about who committed a crime but never about the lotto numbers?

- I don't know. I'd like to. We need to speak to them. Ask Clarkson more forthright questions. Be more specific. He knows something.

- Yes. Sounds reasonable. How about you give me forty-five to fifty minutes.

- Sounds good. I'm at the café near the motel.

The phone call goes quiet.

- Hello? You still there?, I ask.

Rita says - Yeah. The café, they got a TV?

I look around the café. There is one on a wall.

- Yeah. Why?

- Remember when our plan was to talk to Matthew Trenton and Chad again?, asks Rita.

- Yeah.

- Put it on Channel 4, says Rita.

I motion to the café person to put the TV on. They nod. I hold my hand up showing four fingers. The café person changes the channel to 4. There is the front of a familiar looking house. Down the road from the house are a heap of flashing blue and red lights. Some uniforms unreeling crime scene tape. There is a body on under a white plastic tarp. I've caught the end of the report as the journalist says that's all we have for now.

- What the fuck? That house looks familiar. Was that Clarkson Glennis's house?, I say noticing the barista look at me with that silent look of watch the language please.

- Yep. How 'bout I come get you now and we go to Clarkson's house and see what this is all about.

- Sure, my mind wanders away adrift in a thought I have trouble recognising - that sounds good.

- See you in twenty minutes.

I look at the clock.

07:08.

I ask for another cup of coffee. I ask the barista if they have anything harder. They smile. Shake their head no. Coffee it is.

I look at the clock again. It looks like today is starting earlier than planned.

07:09.

Rita Allen

Kids are up. Even when they aren't trying to make noise they are still noisy. I look at the clock on the drawers next to my side of the bed.

06:57.

Can I please sleep past seven for once as an adult?

I look at my husband. Asleep. I don't know how he manages to stay asleep when the kids are up. I wake up when I hear them turn in bed let alone when they cough or turn the TV on in the morning.

I glance at my clock again.

06:58.

I rub my eyes and yawn. I lie on my back and look at the ceiling. I turn the TV we have at the end of our bed on. My husband stirs.

- What? Turn that off. It's got to be four in the morning.

- It's nearly seven, I tell him.

He groans and pulls the quilt over his head to block out the light.

My phone rings. I look at my clock.

06:59.

Who is ringing at this time of the day?

Natalie.

I answer - It's not even seven yet what do you want?

While we're talking I hear the news on the TV. I only hear snippets. TV says body found. Near the home. Natalie mentions being at a café. Clarkson Glennis. Successful children's show producer.

I ask Natalie if the café has a TV and tell her to turn it to channel 4.

We're both silent as we watch the last bit of the story.

Another body found at the front of the house owned by someone who is now a person of interest. Who is the body? I don't say anything. I'm fairly certain it's going to be one of two people.

- What the fuck? That house looked familiar. Was that Clarkson Glennis's house?, says Natalie.

 - Yep, I say - How 'bout I come get you now and we go to Clarkson's house and see what this is all about.

Natalie says something sounding as though her mind is a thousand miles away.

- See you in twenty minutes.

I get out of bed and start dressing.

- Leaving already?, My husband asks.

- Another body.

- This fucking town.

I don't disagree with him. I lean over my husband and kiss him on the check.

- See you later tonight.

As I'm walking out the door I get a call from Detective Inspector James Rawls. Who wants an update and right before hanging up, I hear him say – This fucking town.

I don't disagree.

Natalie Fenix

7:29.

I hear a car horn beep twice. I look out the window of the cafe and in her car waits Rita. I clip my gun to my belt. Clip my badge to my trouser pocket and put my phone in my pocket. I open the car door, take my seat and put on the belt.

Before I've even clipped the belt closed Rita says - We got some serious things to sort out here.

- Serious?, I ask.

Rita says - Rawls called. Wants an update. Wants to know what leads we have. Wants to know who we've spoken to. Wants to know who we're going to speak to.

- He wants a report of what we've done and where we're going?, I respond.

- Yep, says Rita.

- I heard he likes dot points, I say.

Rita scoffs, and smiles then says - Better start writing.

We get to Clarkson Glennis' house. There some squad cars with lights flashing. A police van is parked halfway up the driveway. Some curious by-stander's watching the goings on. A handful of journalists stand next to their vans. Jotting notes or thoughts into their notebooks. Getting a story ready. Trying to make sense of the world. Trying to figure out a way to communicate to the masses what is happening. I see Rita nod towards the journalist's. I see Ebony Bowen next to her camera man.

Rita parks the car and we get out. We make our way to where the body is. It's impossible to hide a giant blue tarp. I look under the tarp.

- Fuck.

Rita goes - Who?

I say - Matthew Trenton.

We both stand silent.

Rita says - I better give them something.

- Give who something?, I ask.

Rita nods her head towards the pack of journalists.

- Oh, I say.

Rita walks away. I stand where Matthew's body lies. Staring at the blue tarp. Willing it to give me answer. Instead it throws up the picture of an innocent face. I close my eyes. Take a breath. I open my eyes.

I walk over to where Rita is talking to the journalists. One of them, Ebony Bowen, looks at me. Neither of us say or do anything.

Rita is asked a question. She looks at me. I nod. A few words later, Rita finishes her statement and we walk away from the media throng.

- There goes one lead, I say.

We head towards the police van in the driveway. We are almost at the police van when Rawls sticks his head out the back of a police van and spot's us.

- Good, in here you two, he orders.

We step into the back of the police van. There are four or five other people in there and it's a bit crowded.

Rawls continues - The house has a few security cameras pointing away from the front of the house to down the driveway where the victim's body was found. We're about to watch what the camera captured over the past couple of hours.

Rita says - Hopefully something good.

There are a few clicks of a mouse. The hard drive whirls into action. Some more mouse clicks. The van smells like it hasn't been used for a while. Bleach crossed with take-away food.

The person controlling the computer goes - Okay, here we go. Some movement over here.

They point to a van driving into shot. The van stops. Then the back door opens. We can't see anyone but can clearly see a human being pushed out the back of the van. The van door closes and the van drives off.

Our boss points to someone in the van - You, go walk around the neighbourhood, see if you can spot any other cameras around that area.

There are some more mouse clicks.

The person controlling the computer says - That's it, until the person who found the body walks by.

They point at the screen.

- Rewind and zoom in on the van, I ask.

After a few mouse clicks we have a fairly close up view of the van. It's a bit out of focus but the sign on the van is quite clear. On the side it says 'Secant Line Exteriors'.

Rawls says - What the hell is a secant line?

I'm not sure who says it but someone says - It's a line that intersects a curve at least twice. Comes from the Latin word *secare* which means to cut.

Rawls goes - Give me an example.

- A line that goes through a circle, the same person replies.

I look at Rita. We both heard it. Circle. We immediately look to the person operating the security camera software.

Rita says - Rewind, is there a better view of the van. Number plates. Any kind of unique identifiable marks?

Rawls, almost demanding - Got something here? Spill it. What the hell does a secant line have to do with anything.

I say - It's not the secant line. It's the circle.

- Circle? As in that group of people who supposedly do shit they shouldn't? Is that where you're going with this?

I say - Yes, those very people.

- And the victim, they are part of the Circles. Was he a suspect?

Rita says - I wouldn't say suspect but definitely someone who may have information that pointed us in a certain direction.

- What direction is that?

I say - After a few other enquiries, the direction of Clarkson Glennis.

Rawls doesn't say a thing. He looks at me. Then at Rita. He looks back at the security camera footage playing on the computer. He takes moment to compose himself.

The person who went looking for other cameras in the area comes back into the van. We stop and look at them. They shake their heads, no other cameras.

There is a brief pause.

Rawls eventually speaks - What the fuck are you two talking to Clarkson Glennis for? Do you know how many favours from our political leaders he has in his back pocket?

Rita and I don't say or do anything.

- Enough to fucking end the careers of half the people in this city. Yeah, I've heard the stories about the Circles. And I know enough

about police work and the law that you don't go throwing dumb-
founded accusations around and at people like Clarkson Glennis.

- We spoke to him already, I say.

- Did he say much? Give up any fantastic leads did he?

- No, I say.

- That's why you get good information before you go see
someone like him.

Rita says - We did have some information. The other enquires
directed us to him.

- Oh yeah? Who?

Rita replies - Chad, err, you'd know him best as Simple Chad.

- I know that person. I know how unreliable he is. Why, would
either of you, think speaking to him was good?

- The victim under the tarp sent us his way, I say.

- Now look at where the victim is, Rawls says gesturing with his
arms to outside where Matthews's body is being loaded into the
back of the coroners van.

- Do we think Chad here might be someone we should go bring
back to the station for further discussions about the homicide of the
victim? What's his real name anyway? No matter, go get Chad. Bring
him back to the station. And let's start doing this right shall we? Not
only do we have a young child to locate but now we got another
homicide. Go on get.

Rawls does the see you later thing with his hand.

Then he says - Wait. Why don't you two focus on finding
Mitchell Winters. I'll get some other detectives to focus on this
homicide investigation.

- I'm murder police but okay, says Rita.

We walk out back to the car. Rawls follows us.

- Seriously, what have you two got here? This Matthew Trenton got anything to do with Mitchell Winters?

I say - No.

Rita adds - We don't think Chad does either but we're all but sure they both know who does.

- So now what?, asks Rawls.

I say - Let us go speak with Chad again. We'll see if we can get anything more out of him. Maybe another name. Then whoever is investigating Matthew Trenton's murder can take him back to the station for that. But let us speak first.

Rawls thinks it over. Starts nodding his head - Ok. Go speak to him. See what he says.

And much to my disappointment, myself and Rita go to speak to Chad.

Twice in two days.

The dark opens wider and feeds further. I need light but I know it's still distant. Still that little bit out of reach. That object in the future I walk towards but don't seem to be getting any closer. Then I remember something. And just as quickly I push that memory back to the bottom.

We get in Rita's car and drive to Chad's house.

I don't know it yet, but later, it's this moment in time I look back on and conclude it was a moment of no return.

One side of a shape sightly closer to the middle than the other side.

Ebony Bowen

I am woken up by the sound of my mobile ringing. I sit up and see Cary lying beside me. What fucking bullshit decisions has my brain made on my behalf? I thought we were done with this kind of thing.

I answer the phone - Hello?

It's Dennis. Who sounds like he hasn't taken a breathe for a few hours but somehow manages to spit out - Get to the house owned by Clarkson Glennis A.S.A.H.F.P.

- Clarkson Glennis?

- Grab whoever you need to operate a camera. Get a van from the station and get ready to broadcast live. It's another body. Two bodies and one missing child. The legs of this story keep growing. Did you find anything else out yesterday at the shopping centre? Get to that house and get that story on the tape.

The phone call ends before I even get a word out.

I put my phone back on the bedside table. I rub my eyes. I need coffee.

Then I need another one.

But first. Cary. I remember not getting far with the people at the shopping centre so we drove around and ended up getting dinner. We said our goodbyes. Then we ended up going back to my place.

Fucking hell.

I nudge Cary.

- Yes, what?

- Get up. We got go do a story.

- This early? Where we going?

- The house of Clarkson Glennis.

- You mean the producer guy? That Clarkson Glennis?

- Yes, now get dressed and lets go.

We get up. Get dressed and get out to the van. Which we were supposed to drop off back to the station but, well, other things happened. We get in the van.

- Can we stop somewhere to get a quick coffee?, asks Cary.

- That goes without saying.

In the van neither of us say anything. We get our coffee's and drink in silence. It is not uncomfortable. We make our way to Clarkson Glennis' house. In my mind I am mulling over several things. The body from yesterday. The missing child. Another body this morning. The police will treat them all as separate incidents. Media will speculate.

The game cycles through its motions.

Again.

We get to Clarkson Glennis' House. We can see where the body is. There is a tarp covering the area where the body, no doubt, lies.

Cary says - This looks like it going to be a fun day already.

If only we had the foresight or clairvoyance to know what would be coming our way. We might very well stay in the van. Drive away. Sort out once and for all what the fuck is going on between us.

Live our lives.

But we don't, so we get out and get ready to send a live story back to the newsroom.

Outside the van is a little chaotic. Some other news teams are jostling for attention. Asking the onsite officers what happened? Who is the victim? Can you give any details?

The police will say nothing until they know for sure.

I see Rita and the other detective behind the tape. Rita watches.

The other detective takes a peak under the tarp. Puts the tarp down. Stands up. Looks at Rita. I can't hear what is said but I can make out the single word from lip reading. It is unmistakable.

Fuck.

This story just grew another set of legs.

I ask Cary - Are you ready with the camera and sound.

Cary gives a single word answer - Yes.

I hope we are not going to have one of those days.

It will be worse. Far worse. But we don't know that yet.

- Rita. RITA?

I get her attention. She walks over.

- Well, you sure picked a day, she says.

- Tell me about it. Should've seen this morning before Cary and I got here.

Cary scoffs.

- Who's the body?, I ask.

- Ahh, can't say for now.

- So you know who it is?

Some other journalists stick there microphones out. Another camera man stands the other side of me.

Rita sees what's going on and puts her hands up in a defensive pose - Until the body is confirmed, we are unable to say. Right now, we have a body, who is known to police, foul play is suspected, we are unsure if it relates to any other case currently under investigation.

- What cases are they?, asks another journalist.

- I am unable to provide that information at the moment.

Rita's detective partner walks over but stand just outside of frame.

I look at her. She at me. There is no nod, no smile and no acknowledgement between us. Just an awareness the other is there.

- Can you tell us how the victim died?, asks that same journalist.

Rita turns to her partner, who nods her head.

- Severe blunt force trauma to the back of the head. The single blow would have caused instantaneous death. That's all we're willing to say for now. We are looking at nearby residences to see if there was any security camera footage which may shed some light.

With that Rita walks off and talks to the other detective. I don't hear everything, but I'm certain I hear 'There goes one lead.'

Which seems an innocent enough comment, but one lead to what? The body this morning? Mitchell? Something else?

Cary says - Get your words sorted, I'll get a clip-mic ready for the cross.

We have always worked well together, but for the most part, it has never translated well outside of work.

Maybe I need to make some changes. Figure something out.

Maybe Cary needs to do the same.

Maybe we'll do that later.

For now, we need to speak to Clarkson Glennis. I start walking to his front door. They are wooden. There are two of them. It's like an entrance to a castle. Or a church.

It's an ominous looking entry.

Chapter 8

I would turn some music on but what's the point? When you don't
exist everything sounds the same. There is some relief at expending
with Circle Conformist Fuck Number One. As they say; possession
is nine tenths of the law. And seeing as I'm no longer in possession
of Circle Conformist Fuck Number One that means I'm nine tenths
of the law innocent. Which is pretty good odds if you think about it
which I'm pretty sure you can't. Or won't. Or whatever. Or
something else.

I reach under my driver's seat and what I'm looking for is there.
Taped up nice and safe. I grab it. I hold it in my hand and remove
the excess tape. I stick it behind by back into the belt and trousers.
What this gun does will compliment Circle Conformist Fuck
Number Two. Also known as Simple Chad for those of you who are
having trouble keeping up with the narrative. After this, I'm going to
give the gun to someone and advise them, very strongly, that they
need to do something they probably should have done a long time
ago. I went to Circle Conformist Fuck Number Two's house once. I
think or maybe I just heard about it. I am not looking forward to the
visit. At least it will be short. Do what I will then leave. As good as
plan as any. If there were any plans to begin with. Which there
probably weren't. I can't remember. This all just feels like something
that's part of whatever the technical word for reality is.

I drive. At least that's what I think I'm doing. I need to focus on this
chapter. My thoughts move forward to the next. I'm looking
forward to the next. There is a lot to say. A lot to be heard. But

Circle Conformist Fuck Number Two needs to be dealt with. They, and Circle Conformist Fuck Number One, shone a light on something that needed to stay dark.

I keep thinking I'm driving.

Past roads. Past houses. Past shops. Past alleyways. Past intersections. Past signs. Past something else. Past I don't know what it is. Past or something.

I notice I'm rocking backwards and forwards in my seat. We must be getting close to Circle Conformist Fuck Number Two's house. I check the glovebox for a cloth to use as a mask. I grab it and wrap it around my non-existent hand to make sure I don't forget the cloth. I'm all but certain this place is going to be covered in shit. As a matter of fact, I'm totally certain this place is going to be covered in shit. I turn a corner and then another one. I drive a bit and see where I'm going. I drive by. I look at the various neighbour's houses. Not much seems to be going on. I get to the end of the road and u-turn to go back. I stop a house before the house I'm going to. I pull the gun out the back of my pants and check it's loaded.

It is.

I put the gun back. I hold the cloth over my face and walk to the house I'm going to. As I'm getting closer I start to notice a foul smelling odour. Has a neighbour even complained about this? What other foul smelling odour is this foul smelling odour overshadowing? I get to the door and notice it's slightly ajar. I knock. I wait. I knock again. I wait again.

No answer.

I push through the door and then it hits me. The smell still reeks through the cloth I'm holding. I should have got some eye coverings as the smell is burning my eyes. If I had eyes, they would be starting to water. Which they are. There are no lights on but the natural light is enough to show the bench tops, tables; basically anything with a horizontal surface, no scratch that, any surface; be it vertical or upside down is covered in shit. Fresh shit. Dried shit. Shit stains. I'm pretty sure it's all animal shit but if it was tested and human shit particles were found. It would not be a surprise.

At all.

I decide the cloth I'm holding over my face will work better if I tie it up. I see a two litre plastic bottle of what could have been cola. It could have been lemonade which has turned black due to the length of time it had been sitting there. I pick the bottle up and unscrew the lid. It smells like cola and whiskey. Cola and whiskey is a slightly more palatable odour than what is currently available. On a nearby table is a box of tissues. I stand there for a minute shoving tissue after tissue into the bottle. I empty the tissue box and decide that will be enough. The tissue has absorbed the cola and whiskey mixture. It will work for what I am going to use it for. I shake the bottle and bits of wet tissue stick to the side of the bottle. Making it slightly sound proof. I jam the bottle over the muzzle of my gun. I look at the couches and seats around the place. I grab a cushion that it is partly clean. I move through the house looking for Circle Conformist Fuck Number Two. I look in various rooms. There are some cats who don't looked impressed. Another room has a small dog that is lying in the corner of the room. It looks up at me. Barks once. Realises the effort is too much and puts its head back down. I walk on through. Past the toilet and shower. I keep going through the hallway where I make it to a kitchen slash dining room area. On the kitchen floor lie's Circle Conformist Fuck Number Two. I look at the bottle on the end of my gun. Circle Conformist Fuck Number Two drank the rest and is now passed out on the floor of his kitchen. I yell out at him.

No answer.

I kick him in the stomach. Some vomit rolls out his mouth. I kick him again. He sort of wakes up and mumbles something. Probably no. Or stop. Or hey. Or something else. I kick him again. Harder. I yell at him to wake up. He stirs a bit. Spits some leftover vomit out his mouth and looks up.

His eyes open wider. Alert. That sub-conscious part of the brain, if it even exists, throwing out hormones telling the rest of the body to wake the fuck up.

He slurs – What are you doing here?

He takes a breath and spits some more. He nods. I think that's what moving your head up and down is called.

He says – Nothing I can say to change what is going to happen?

I don't say a thing. Or I say no. I'm not sure. I kick him in the stomach again. More vomit rolls out.

I go to kick him again but he deflects the kick and says – Alright, fuck. Stop it already.

I stand there. Looking at the pitiful fuck. I might feel sorry for him if I existed but since I don't, I don't.

He says – Well? Is there something else?

No.

He says – So?

I point my gun with the bottle at the end at his face. I hold the cushion in front of the bottle. I pull the trigger. Cola and whiskey spits out over the wall. My pants. The floor. The cushion I'm holding. The end of the bottle is shattered and bits of tissue fall to the ground. Some of the filling used to stuff the cushion covers Circle Conformist Fuck Number Two's face. Other parts of the cushion lie on the ground. Turning red. I look at my pants. They are covered in cola and whiskey. The very bottom of the pants is spattered with blood along with my shoes. I put cushion behind the spot where the head of Circle Conformist Fuck Number Two used to be. I rip what's left of the bottle off the gun and drop it on the floor. I turn around and leave. As I walk by the room where the dog is I notice it hasn't moved. Not at all concerned with what just happen. It's almost like its fucking grateful that it happened. I can't see any of the cats. I am leaving Circle Conformist Fuck Number Two here meaning this house is ten tenths of the law in possession of Circle Conformist Fuck Number Two. Which suits me fine. I walk outside and away from the house to my van. I drive off to my next stop. I take the cloth of my face and notice there are fine spots of blood on it. I throw it out the window. I'm going to have a shower. I remember I have a friend waiting. It's nice to know someone is there waiting for you. But the nice thought leaves as soon as I remember I have another stop to make.

Which if I remember correctly is something I am looking forward to doing.

Or it's something I need to do.

Or it's something else.

8

Bekka walked into the lounge from and saw Annie and David both on the couch. They looked asleep. She remembered them doing a similar thing when they were younger. Long before Mitchell was even a thought. She smiled. Then remembered why she was there and stopped. Annie heard Bekka enter the room and opened her eyes.

- Sleep much?, Bekka asked.

- Not a second, Annie responded.

David heard and opened his eyes - Me neither.

The TV was on but the volume was down. Bekka flicked the TV to the news channel which was partway into a story about a body that was found near the house of well-known TV producer Clarkson Glennis. On the TV was Ebony Bowen summarising what was happen.

- Annie. David. Wake up, said Bekka.

- What's wrong?, said Annie.

David looked straight at the TV. He didn't recognise the house in the background but he knew something had happened at a house of someone well known. It was that type of house. All three listened as Ebony Bowen finished her report.

… police say the body was found by a passer-by
earlier this morning. There are no details on who
the deceased is but a police spokesperson has
stated they were known to police. The owner
of the house, media entity Clarkson Glennis,
commented it is coincidental that a body was

found just metres from their house. Police
are scouring camera footage taken from
nearby residences for possible information.
Police have asked anyone with any
information to contact them immediately.
For now, Ebony Bowen, Channel 4 news.

Annie immediately sat upright. She looked around. David stood up from the couch and watched Annie looking for something.

Bekka asked - What are you looking for?

- A card. A card with a phone number. The one the detective gave us at the station.

David knew the card and started looking around the lounge for the card.

After Annie and David fell asleep last night, Bekka had taken it upon herself to clear some rubbish and dishes from the lounge. There was no card on the table. Then she remembered the card stuck to the fridge with a magnet. She went and got it. She held it out.

- Is the card?

Annie looked at it and her eyes widened - Yes. That's it.

She took it from Bekka. Grabbed a phone and called the number. There was a slight delay as Annie waited for her phone call to be answered. Eventually someone answered.

- Hi, this is Annie Winters, Mitchell's mum. We just saw the news report. Does that have anything, err, is there any news on Mitchell?

Both David and Bekka could hear someone answering Annie's question but they couldn't make out anything. Annie said yes or okay or yep; or some variation on all three. The longer the phone call went the more Annie slouched. David and Bekka watched. They knew the news wasn't exactly what they wanted.

Annie eventually said - Thanks for the update.

Both David and Bekka looked at Annie waiting for her to give them an update. Annie sat down on the couch before she spoke.

- They don't have any news on Mitchell. They said the person they found at the house was known to police. If they get anymore news or have an update they will call. So basically what the news report said.

All three disappointed that the police would not embellish further. It was David and Annie's kid that was missing. Surely that meant they could get some information the news couldn't.

It didn't.

It meant they would get only what the police wanted to tell them. Which in this case was exactly what the police told the news.

The wind was knocked out of all three of them.

Bekka walked into the kitchen and put the kettle on. She didn't ask David or Annie if they wanted tea or coffee she was going to make the usual for all three of them. It seemed selfish but Bekka needed a moment of familiarity. Getting all three of them their usual would have to suffice. She noticed the silence in the house. Sure the TV was on but the volume was low. There was an occasional chirp of a bird. A crack of the house expanding under the light of the morning sun. A car driving by. Bekka went about getting everyone a morning coffee.

David looked out the window at the sunlight. It wasn't as bright as it should be. David wondered how bright it should be.

Bekka brought back their coffees and handed a cup each to Annie and David.

Annie stared into her coffee mug. Debating. Thinking. Trying not to do either. It was hard to get a read on Annie. It was as though Annie possessed some special barrier that deflected any concern heading in Annie's direction.

Bekka sat in a nearby couch. All three were silent. The morning's news report had promise but failed to deliver.

It all felt like a Nick Cave song. Love; murder. Determination; confusion. Life; death. Silence; noise. Hope; despair. Beginning; end.

Annie set her coffee mug on the coffee table in front of the couch then rested her head on her forearms and closed her eyes. Annie wouldn't sleep; hadn't slept.

David kept looking out the window. Still wondering how bright the sunlight should be. There wouldn't be an answer. David sort of nodded to himself internally. The sunlight was as bright as it was. And that's as bright as it would ever be. David got up from the couch. Picked up Annie's coffee mug. His. And took Bekka's from her. David went into the kitchen and washed them. It was the first domestic like thing David had done since Mitchell went missing. David didn't know what to make of it. So he went back to lounge room and sat on the couch next to Annie. David looked at Bekka who was scratching the back of her hand. David didn't know why and looked at Annie.

What to do about Annie?

An answer wasn't found. Never had David seen Annie like this. Sure Annie had been disappointed at various times in her life. There were times Annie had lost her job and couldn't find one for an extended length of time. That was always demoralising. One of Annie's childhood friends had died early of some medical condition. David couldn't remember what the condition was called. He could remember not being able to pronounce it properly.

But he had never seen Annie like this. This was something else.

David realised Annie probably thought the same about how he was acting.

A news break appeared on the TV. All three of them eyes wide open. Annie grabbed the TV remote and turned the volume up. It was the same as earlier. Body found near church. There was a short sport section about the various events and games that were going on in the afternoon. A few frames and words about the weather for the rest of the day. Then it was over. The TV resumed normal programming.

Annie turned the TV volume down and put the remote back we she picked it up from. Which was on the floor right in front of where she was sitting on the couch.

Bekka leaned back in her chair. She had never seen Annie like this either. There was some concern nestled way back in her thoughts. Bekka was ready to step up but she had faith in her sister. She knew Annie. It might take a while and she might never be what she was but Bekka knew Annie would, perhaps not move on, but certainly deal with what happened.

Somehow.

David she wasn't so sure about. Bekka was pretty certain that David would take Annie's lead. It provided some comfort for Bekka.

- When did you say your parents were going to be here?, asked David.

- This afternoon, later tonight depending on cars on the road. How often they had to stop. That kind of thing, replied Bekka.

All three of them sat, waited, and listened to the silence in the house.

Children make a hell of a lot of noise.

Chapter 9

I drive up the driveway and park just a bit from the front of the house. Or church. Or some other type of grotesque building covered with ornate architectural exaggerations. When buildings are this big, this grand, this delusional; it's hard to tell the difference. I'm just going to call it a house. It's either the house of Grayson Bell. Or the house of God.

I have problems with both of them.

I know there are security cameras but they do not worry me. The house, large and sprawling as it is, never fails to induce a feeling of sickness inside me. Or another feeling I don't know the name of. Or perhaps something entirely different. Or who knows?

I remember the house from a young age. I don't remember before that. And what I remember of the house I'm not sure. I just remember the house. Memory as a form of unreliable narrative. Or unreliable meta-narrative. Which depends on if memory is even a thing. I think memory is just a hoax. What we remember is what we want; not what was. Or is. Or were. Or this. Is this even a word?

After a few steps I finally make it to the door. I reach my hand up to knock then think better of it. I take a step back and with my leg, I'm sure that's what they're called, I kick the door. It careens back into the wall. The door handle makes a round dent on the plastered wall. I hear someone yell out. The voice unmistakeable. The voice I've known the longest.

The voice says Who's that? Who's there?

I don't say anything. If I could I'd say you know who it is.

The voice responds oh you. I was waiting for this. The news and all.

The voice walks out from a room and there, standing, which is generally what people do when they're standing, is Grayson Bell. One time foster parent. One time worse thing that ever happened to me. Or maybe not. Or maybe best thing. Or thing that was going to happen regardless. Nature versus nurture where neither wins and some unidentified force is in control.

What news? I say if I could.

The news. On the TV. You know who I'm talking about. I asked you to do that.

I stand there. I get a brief flash of pushing something out the back of my van. I nod. Not so much in agreeance but more to keep the conversation going. I have no need to explain any detail of what did or might not have happened.

I need my freedom I say. I can't keep doing this for you so you stay out of the light. I'm going to end up in the light if it keeps up.

Grayson smirks. Like he knows something I don't. Figured out something I haven't. Or done something. Or did something else.

You're more free than you imagine says Grayson. I took you from your home. You were not going to be whatever your mother wanted you to be. You had no chance. But, unlike the others we had like you, you made it through. Made a mockery of the living and dead alike. You need to do what you are here for. Then leave.

That night, when I saw the scar on the arm I knew who it was. Something triggered inside of me. Or would have if I existed. It was fear. Joy. Anger. Violence. Catharsis. An ending. Another choice. I couldn't help it. I made the choice. I followed him. Watched him. Stayed patient. When the time was right. I fucking caved in his head with a crowbar. Then I burn't him with a DVD. A copy of the very one I am on. I felt happy. And if I felt happy after that, I thought, how much happier would I feel if I did that to all the others?

He was the one who grabbed you to begin with. You were just standing there. Where was your mother? Your father? says Grayson.

That is what I remember the most. That scar. After that is a blur.

Yeah, you blacked out. I didn't think he was going to do that.

Who put me in the hospital? I ask.

A look of pain comes across Grayson's face. As though the one question he didn't want to answer was that one.

I'm going to say a name, he says, and it will be the second to last time I say this name. I will only say the name. Nothing else. If you have questions following that name I will have no answers.

It's like he is waiting for me to say something like ok.

Well I say.

Clarkson Glennis.

I don't get angry. I don't punch a hole into the wall. I don't push Grayson over. I stand there. Emotionless. Speechless. Thoughtless. Which is no surprise considering I don't exist. Clarkson Glennis. I've been keeping the light pure for that fucking stuck up fuck.

Grayson, aware of the silence, says when you've got dirt on someone who has the same dirt on you, there is a mutual desire for self-preservation. In your case, you were the dirt I had on someone.

And what dirt was on you? I ask.

You. Grayson says.

It doesn't register. Or it does. Grayson goes on with what he is saying before I can reply.

I should have spoken up. I didn't. My lack of speaking out is an act

of being complicit says Grayson. Complicit is a sin of silence. I can
longer be complicit. When I saw that person in the news. I knew the
door was closing. If I didn't act quickly other doors would close. I
needed one to stay open. Which is why I asked you to clear the air.
To rid the world of those whose sin is unforgivable.

And what dirt is on me? I ask further.

Grayson opens his mouth to say something. Stops. Coughs a little to
clear his throat and says what happened to you is a blemish on the
world. Not society. Not a demographic. On all of us. A decision was
made to keep you outside those societies. Those demographics. It
was decided that you have a freedom the rest of us can never have.

What freedom is that? I query.

In the most straightforward way possible, with no inflection or
change of tone Grayson says you simply don't exist. On paper
anyway. You have no records stored in a government archive. No
records stored anywhere. You have total freedom.

I take in that statement and draw out two ideas. I don't exist. I have
total freedom. Some people who think they're smart and like to say
life is complicated. They are not that smart.

Nor complicated.

I think deep down we both knew this moment had to happen and how this was going to turn out. Inevitability is unavoidable. The inevitable is identifiable before it happens. Grayson sighs.

I reach to behind my back and pull out the gun. I hand it to Grayson. He takes it. Looks at it. As if he has never seen a gun before.

Is it loaded? he asks.

No. I say.

He hands the gun back. I pull back the slide so a bullet can enter the chamber. I hand it back.

Saftey's off I say.

Grayson nods. Puts the gun in one of the pockets of his robe. Pauses. Looks at me. Trying to say something to me but unable. If I existed I might feel a bit of remorse for what's going to happen. But I don't. I say nothing. Give no instruction. I don't know how but Grayson always knew in advance at anything I was about to do. He bought my house outside the usual channels. Gave it to me. I didn't know how to respond. There were no hugs. No thanks. I just took the keys out of his hand and went inside. He nodded, got into his car and drove off. I haven't told him what the inside of the house looks like. If he wants to know he can read what I said earlier in chapter two.

I say I'll see myself out.

There is no response. Grayson turns and walks back into the room he walked out of when I arrived.

Knowing the layout of the house well, I go to the room where the security cameras are monitored. I see the laptop controlling all. I go to the anti-virus software and unclick a few settings such as automatically back-up to the cloud when cameras are disabled. I clear the cache. I remove all the temporary files. I click a few spots and the cameras are disabled. I shut them off. I disconnect them from the wireless network. I shut down the wireless network. I find where the digital copies are stored on the C Drive. I go to that folder and delete all. I go to the install/uninstall programs place. I uninstall the security camera software. I uninstall the drivers. Finally, I move to the restore factory settings option. I hover the mouse over OK. I pause a second. Or maybe it was less. Or it was longer.

I click OK.

There is another are you sure message. I don't pause this time.

I click OK.

The laptop starts turning over. There are some sounds. And on the screen it has 1%. I wait. It goes to 3%. Then 6%. Then 7%. It stays on 7% for a little while then goes to 12%. I see that a non-sequential pattern is emerging. I turn and walk out the room. Get to my van and drive off.

I got to get home. Shower. Eat food, if that's what it's called. See if my friend is doing alright. I have to drop off something to a certain TV station.

Just like the laptop, my past is now erased. Any link will soon be gone. I won't be a stat in a census. Or an entry in the births, deaths and marriages register. There are no records of my schooling. No dental records. No tax file number. No social security receipts.

There will be nothing.

I won't exist.

Just like how I don't exist now.

Ebony Bowen

I get back to the office. This morning was a bit hectic. Another dead body to start the day. A child still missing. Establishment types doing all they can too neither deny nor confirm. I throw my bag in the bottom draw of my desk and slouch into my chair. I sit there for a minute. Eyes closed. Head resting in my hands. I hear the other people in the office doing their work. There is a strange sense of rhythm in the noise. The underlying beat of employment. The sound of a factory not to dissimilar. I remember this morning. What else will today bring?

I don't know where Cary went. Probably to change battery packs for the camera. Apart from getting a fact wrong, the worst nightmare for a journalist (especially TV based journalists) is running out of charge for the camera. It hasn't happened to me yet. Cary is always making sure that never happens. If only he was as reliable in other areas of our life.

The phone on my desk rings.

- Ebony Bowen.

The voice on the other end says - Hi Ebony. It's Alicia at the reception desk. There is a courier here with a delivery for you. Says only you can sign for it.

- Ok. I'll make way over.

I hang up the phone, grab a pen and make way to Alicia's desk.

It's a short walk. I get to Alicia's desk. We wave hello at each the other. The courier doesn't look like a normal courier. Something else. Wearing the same kind of hi-vis shirts as other couriers. I think nothing of it. I look for a badge of a courier company on the shirt. There isn't one. The courier hands over a small electronic device.

- Just an initial will be fine, the courier says.

I initial 'EB'. The courier hands over an envelope.

- Thanks, I say.

- I can't remember the last time I was here, the courier says - must have been years ago. Maybe when I was a kid. Life moves fast. Or moves at a normal pace. Or I don't know.

I give one of those friendly smiles that means I can hear what you say, but I have other things I need to go do. There is something odd about this courier.

- I'm sorry, what courier company are you with?

- I work on contract. Self-employed. Last time I was here, had to have been when I got a bit lost. I don't remember much. A mechanic looking person found me. Had a bandage on his arm. You could see the cut. He helped.

I keep smiling - Got to love a good samaritan.

The courier doesn't react. Just says - Yeah, good samaritan. Then he walks out the station.

- What is it?, Alicia asks.

- Not sure, I respond.

On the front of the package, in child-like scribble, is my name with my work address. I open the package. In a clear case is a disc. It's a DVD. I know it's a DVD because on the disc is printed DVD-r. There is no hand writing on it. Just the brand name of the disc and how much information it can record. In this case 120 minutes or 4.7GB. There is another disc. This one looks like someone set fire to it. I turn it over in my hand. It isn't getting played. The other one does not look damaged at all.

Alicia looks at the discs then at me. She wants to know what's on the playable disc.

So do I.

I say - Let's go find out what's on the disc.

She presses a button on the phone on her desk. Probably diverting it or putting the out of office message up. Alicia follow's me to an editing room. On our way there we run into Cary.

- Battery packs all charged and/or replaced, he says.

- Good work, I say.

I show him the disc. Cary nods and walks to an editing room. We go into the room and shut the door. It's a small room but the three of us fit in easy. Cary sits at the editing desk. Myself and Alicia take a seat either side of Cary. Cary loads the disc into the player. He opens the viewing software on the editing suite. It loads to the first frame and pauses. Cary clicks on the play icon on the screen. It starts off black. We can hear voices.

- Where is he?

- Over here.

There is a rustling sound. What sounds like footsteps. There is some banging like something got dropped. Steel on concrete.

- He tied up?

The black screen disappears. The camera focuses. In. Out. In. Out. It's old camera footage. Looks like it was recorded on videotape to begin with then converted to digital and saved to this disc. The sound crackles. You can hear what's happening in the video but there is an ongoing hiss. The camera finally gets in focus. In a chair is a child. About ten years old. Maybe nine, no older than thirteen. He looks terrified.

- Look at the camera, a voice off screen says.

The child doesn't look.

- Look at the fucking camera, the same voice says louder. Angrier.

A man comes on screen and bangs the arm rests of the chair the child is sitting in. He uses a crowbar.

He has a bandage on his arm.

Fuck. What did that courier say? A man with a bandage?

I want to go back and find out more about the bandage but the screen has our attention. So I keep watching the screen.

- Ok. Ok, the child says and looks at the camera.

I always find it unnerving when someone is looking directly into the camera. It's as though they are looking right at you and somehow looking through you.

- State your name, a voice says off screen. Different from the first two.

- Jayden, says the child. He looks down.

A voice screams - Look at the fucking camera.

The man from before with the crowbar and bandage bangs on the chair again. This time for longer. The kid is in tears and starts screaming. The people off screen start laughing.

I'm not liking where this is going and I say so.

Cary nods.

So does Alicia who sort of mumbles - Yeah.

None of us can stop watching.

It like watching a car accident in slow motion.

From off screen a man walks into frame and stand behind the kid.

- Is that. Is that Clarkson Glennis?, Cary asks.

Alicia squints her eyes and leans in closer to get a better look. I do the same.

- Could be, I say.

I think about it some more. Alicia is nodding her head.

- I think so, I say.

- I think so to, says Alicia.

Clarkson pulls down his pants. I cover my eyes and scream. I open them briefly. A younger person comes on screen. Looks like a thirty year old Grayson Bell. He grabs Clarkson and tries to pull him away from the kid. The man with the crowbar starts beating the thirty year old Grayson Bell lookalike who lets go of Clarkson. Clarkson yells at him to fuck off. The man keeps beating on thirty year old Grayson Bell lookalike until he falls to the ground.

Alicia throws up. Straight onto the ground.

- Stop. Stop the fucking disc Cary, I yell - Now.

Cary stops the disc. The room falls silent. The screen goes black. I want to scream but I cant. I look at Cary. He is white. He turns away and throws up. Alicia is in tears. I rest my hand on her shoulder to offer some sort of support. It seems pointless.

A producer putting together a story for tonight's news in the next editing room opens the door and asks - Is everything is alright?

- No, I say - No. It fucking most definitely is not.

- Why? What is going on?, asks the producer.

- Call the police. Just go call the police, I say.

I lift Alicia up under her arms and lead her out the room. I push the producer out the room.

- Go call the fucking police, I yell at the producer.

I lead Alicia to a nearby seat. Then I go get Cary. Who looks confused in a very bad way.

- Cary.

He doesn't respond.

- Cary let's go, I wave with my hand to come out the room. He looks at me and walks out the room. He sits down next to Alicia. I stand in front of both of them.

- Sit here. Don't move. Don't speak. Don't tell anyone. Wait until the police get here, I tell them.

They both nod. Mouths slightly open. Wanting to say something but saying nothing.

I go to the tearoom. I grab a few bottles of water from the fridge. I give one to Alicia, one to Cary and keep the third for myself. I open mine and take a huge gulp. Cary holds his bottle. Still looking confused. He eventually opens the top. Hands his bottle to Alicia and takes hers. Alicia takes a small sip then a very large sip. Cary opens the bottle and doesn't drink. Just holds it. There is a look of 'What the fuck?' on his face. I've never seen him look like this.

What the fuck does my face look like then?

The producer comes back and says - Police on their way. I also got a senior producer and the ethics officer, whatever you guys just saw needs their involvement. What happened?

- I really don't know but whatever it was it wasn't good, I answer.

The producer nods. They look at Cary and Alicia then takes a seat too wait with us.

We wait. We wait for the police to turn up. The sooner we get that disc out of here. The better. Why was it given to me? What the fuck am I supposed to do about what happened on the disc? I will be asking about Clarkson Glennis. I will find out if thirty year old looking Grayson Bell is in fact Grayson Bell. And once the police see the footage, the man with the bandage will be high on their people we need to speak to list. For now I just need to sit down. Drink some water. That was fucking disgusting. I walk over to the rubbish bin a few feet away. I fall to my knees.

I never want to see what happens after we turned the screen off.

No-one should.

I see the senior producer open the door and start walking to where we are. He can tell something is wrong.

I look at him. We make eye contact. I turn and look the bottom of the rubbish bin. Compared to what I just watched, a rubbish bin has never looked better. A moment of calmness washes over me. I get one comfortable breath in.

Then I throw up and start crying.

Natalie Fenix

Rita says - This guy better tell us something. Smelling that house yesterday, I really don't need to do that again.

This time we prepare. We dab a little of the perfume, which Rita has in the glovebox of the car, above our top lip. We think about it a little more and decide to dab some inside our nostrils.

That place stunk.

We get to Chad's house and park our car in more or less the spot we did last time. As we get closer to the house a familiar smell permeates the air.

Something is dead.

We look around to see if there is a dead cat or bird or dog. Nothing stands out. We keep walking to Chad's house and the closer we get the stronger the smell gets. The closer we get the more we realise what the smell is. We draw our guns and check they are loaded.

Rita signals with her hand to stop. She gets out her phone, calls the station and tells them we got a body. Then she signals with her hand to keep moving. We get to Chad's door. It is open. We both stand either side of the entrance. Rita nods. I raise my gun and step into the house.

- Police, I yell - come out with your hands raised.

Rita follows me. Her gun raised.

We wait a few moments. No-one walks out a room with their hands raised. Nothing bangs against a wall. Nothing falls to the floor. It's quiet. Silence can be a little concerning especially when you expect to hear something. We walk further into the house. We walk by a room. In it, a dog. It doesn't move. Its eyes open watching us. We walk further into the house.

Even with the dab of perfume under and in our noses, the smell is fucking disgusting.

There is a bottle, a soft drink bottle, with its end shredded out. Not sure how, looks like someone very badly cut the end off. We're almost at the kitchen. On the floor are plastic shards, most likely from the bottle, and what looks like small pieces of foam. We eventually make it to the kitchen where we find Chad. Slumped on the ground. There is a giant hole where his head used to be. I see what's happened now.

The soft-drink bottle was used as a makeshift silencer.

Rita says - Looks like someone made a for-one-time use only silencer out of a soft drink bottle and used a cushion to further supress the sound. What's all these black spots? The blood on Chad's shoulders is a dark red. So what's the black spots?

I knell down. I pull a latex glove out my pocket and put it on my left hand. I use a finger to wipe one of those black spots. I smell it.

- It's alcohol and cola, I say.

Rita asks - Well this sucks.

- No doubt Rawls is going to love this escalation in the case.

Rita doesn't say anything. She raises her eyebrows and nods. After a few beats she says - We just got to deal with it. This is police work. If it was easy there'd be no crime.

She crouches down near Chad's body. Tries to figure out a line of shot. She stands and faces Chad. Points her gun out at him and says - Killer stood here. Shooting down. Based on the blood spatter around the body, killer would have copped some spatter.

We look around for footprints. There are a few part footprints but no whole prints. We have to be careful where we step. Rita crouches back down and leans in close to Chad's body. She squints her eyes.

- Looks like someone has kicked and stomped him in the stomach, a few times. Look, there is a print, Rita says while pointing out the print.

I look and there on Chad's body, is a partial footprint.

- Is that vomit?, Rita asks.

I shake my head no. Not that I disagree that its vomit, it's just I don't want to find out. Some things are better left a mystery.

- Let's leave that to the forensics unit, I say - We came here for answers and it looks like we aren't going to get any.

Rita smiles.

- What?, I ask

Rita steps to the corner of the room looking at the ground to Chad's right. Laying there, in its full brass glory, is a shell casing. Rita gets a pen out her pocket, slides the pen into the casing. She picks it up and studies the casing.

- Looks like a .40, Rita says - Originally designed for the FBI, it has now become one the more popular choices for civilians wishing to purchase ammunition for their handguns.

She puts the casing back on the ground where it was picked up from. I lean over and check out the casing. I've seen shell casings like this before. Bullets all look the same but all have their individual markings. I keep looking around to see if there is anything unusual.

Almost everything is unusual. We hear some cars stop out the front.

- That'll be them, says Rita.

She goes to meet them to give a quick rundown on what we have done since we called them.

I look at Chad. Some people, even though recently passed, when you look at their body, a small fragment of their soul stays behind. Attracting the light to guide the spirit to wherever it moves towards. But Chad. No life. No soul. No light. No spirit. It is devoid of anything. All it does it take up space. Even the darkness is staying away.

I hear some voices as they walk up the hallway to where I am. It's Rawls, Rita and a couple of forensics.

Rawls says - This smell is something isn't it?

Rita replies - Hasn't improved since we were last here.

The forensics get to work immediately. One takes photographs. One of them drops yellow evidence markers around the place. The other starts taking swabs of the various stains, liquids, moulds and whatever else.

Rita asks - Any luck on the Secant line sign from the van at the Clarkson Glennis' house?

Rawls goes - None yet. Someone probably got one of those magnetic signs made, puts it on for a reason and takes it off at other times. That line of investigation is bringing up nothing. Bit like this one is now.

I point the casing out to Rawls.

Rawls kneels down and examines the casing - Looks like a .40. Law enforcement the world over use these. Civilian's as well.

Rita asks the question - Are you saying we should be looking closer to home?

- No and I fucking hope not. Can you imagine the shit storm if it turned out it was one of our own who did this?

One of the forensics says - Whiskey.

Rawls thinking about the potential of a shit storm stops and says - Whiskey? What of it? What's its meaning in this context?

The forensic says - Whiskey and coke. That's what these black spots are.

Rawls waves his arms over Chad's body - So how'd they get dispersed in this manner?

The forensic points at the busted soft drink bottle and says - I would suggest that soft drink bottle got used as a silencer and there was still some liquid in the bottle when the shot was taken. Not only the silencer, but it looks like a cushion was also used to supress the noise. Where is the cushion?

We look around. It isn't anywhere.

Rawls looks at us - Taken as a trophy?

Rita responds - Perhaps. This has all been a mess so far. It's just as likely the shooter kept hold of the cushion not realising they were still holding it and just walked away with it.

We keep looking. Then I spot it.

I say - Is that it behind his head?

Everyone looks. The other forensics walks over. Photographs taken before one of them gently pulls what's left of Chad's head forward and removes the cushion. Sure enough, there is a big fucking hole in it.

Rita stands in front of Chad's body like she did before. She holds out one of her arms imitating a gun. With her other arm she pretends to hold the cushion in front of the gun.

The puzzle pieces fit.

Rawls, exasperated, says - What the fuck. Either someone has had some sort of training in killing people or they are really smart with an innate ability to know how to commit crime.

Rita replies - I'm thinking someone from a young age who has been around some pretty fucked up shit. Trained killers wouldn't leave a casing behind. Or part of a bottle they used as a silencer. But this is in line with the violence with the initial body. Something has broken inside our killer and now, whatever was inside, is now outside.

Rawls phone rings. - Hello. Get the fuck out of here. On a DVD? Who is on it? Who? Alright. Put it into evidence. Start making calls. Find out who that kid is.

Rita and I watch him speak. The forensics continue processing the scene. Getting swabs of blood and other liquids. Taking pictures of body's and partial footprints. Dusting for finger prints. They are going to be here a while.

Rawls ends the call and goes - A DVD. A child is abused. Horrifically I'm told. Guess who is on the footage.

Rawls pauses and waits for us to answer his question which we don't.

- One Clarkson Glennis and in the background one, well potentially, one Grayson Bell. There is also a third person but no-one can tell who that is. But, has a bandage on their arm. Kept hitting the chair the child was sitting in with a crowbar.

- What are the chances, that under the bandage is a cut that would become a scar?, I ask.

- Guess what else?, Rawls asks.

- There's more?, I reply.

- Another DVD, this one burnt.

I look at Rita.

- You think the body from yesterday morning is this third person? The man with a bandage?, asks Rita.

- The way this case is working out. I would be surprised if it wasn't.

We look at Rawls. He is thinking it over.

Rita asks - So who do we speak to first?

Rawls goes - If this DVD is anything to go by Clarkson Glennis is done. Go speak to Grayson Bell. Maybe he can shed some light on this.

Rita and I head out of the house and make our way to Grayson Bell's house. Then I remember something.

I yell out to Rawls - That dog, did anyone call RSPCA?

- Go, speak to Grayson, I'll get the dog sorted.

We get in the car and drive away.

Rita goes - Thank fuck we got out that house. That smell was like being killed by a thousand paper cuts. And then being killed again by another thousand cuts in the same place as the first lot.

I couldn't agree more.

Rita Allen

We drive to the front of Grayson Bell's house. Big and sprawling, the house is exactly the kind of house you would think someone devoted to the church wouldn't live in. There is a porch light on but inside the house looks dark.

I shrug and say to Natalie - You never know. No good cop, bad cop deal here. Let's just be straight and ask our questions. Get what we need and go from there. Let's not give this guy any ammunition that might come back on us later.

She nods and says - Yep.

I check my sidearm. Natalie hers. We get out the car and walk to the front door. The door is slightly ajar. It looks like someone has kicked it in. We take a moment to compose ourselves. Although ajar, I knock on the door. There are a few moments of silence then we hear someone walking to the door. The door opens. Standing there is Grayson Bell. He looks at Natalie then at me. Nods his head and sighs.

- Come in, he says.

We go inside the house. I'm a bit taken back at first. Opulent. Posh. Maybe a little pretentious. There is a lot of art which looks expensive. Natalie looks around, eyebrows raised. Not in doubt, perhaps awe. Do church people of Grayson's stature really live in houses like this one?

He points to a room and says - Take a seat. I'll get some tea and coffee.

We walk into the room. One side of the wall is a bookcase full of books. I scan the shelves. The Origin of Species. The Selfish Gene. Ill Fares the Land. No Logo. The Da Vinci Code. The Satanic Verses.

Canterbury Tales. The Illiad. The Divine Comedy. Mrs Dalloway. The Beautiful Struggle. Last Exit to Brooklyn. The Glass Canoe. Go Tell it on the Mountain. The Slap. The End of History. The Wretched of the Earth. Beloved. Legendary Tales of the Australian Aborigines. And so on and so on. There is no TV. No Radio. No computer or laptop. A lone bible sits on the coffee table in the middle of the room. Some art rests on the walls looking back at anyone who looks at them. One of them looks like a Picasso. Other works have a painting style which looks familiar but I can't remember the name of the artist. The art looks like someone used a paint brush to dribble and flick paint onto a canvas. Resting on the tables in the corners of the room are artefacts which appear to be from everywhere in the world. The floor is wooden. Old. Weary. If it could talk who knows what secrets it would spill. I can only imagine what the rest of the house is like.

While Grayson is still out the room I say - I thought the clergy were supposed to live a modest life.

Natalie does not respond.

We hear some clanking of spoons and cups. Grayson Bell walks into the room holding a tray with a jug of steaming water, a smaller jug which probably contains milk, three cups and three spoons. There is no sugar. He sets the tray down next to the bible.

- I was thinking someone such as yourselves would be here sooner or later. I'm surprised at my lack of surprise, says Grayson. He points to the tray - Help yourself.

Natalie gestures to the wider room - Nice collection.

- Mmm, says Grayson - Takes a while to read that many books. For every hour you spend reading, a writer probably spent two or three or more writing.

Natalie and myself look at Grayson Bell. We don't say anything. It's pretty clear why we're here. That doesn't stop me from asking - You know why we're here?

Grayson nods. Looks at the ground. Kind of mumbles - The Circles.

Grayson looks at the art on the wall. At the bookshelf. He walks to the corner of the room and picks up one of the artefacts. Stares at it.

- I got this from Thailand, he says - It's a 530 year old cutting tool.

Natalie asks - Who are the Circle's?

Grayson looks at the artefact some more then puts it back on the table. He turns to face us. He straightens his back and takes a deep breath. Like it's his last.

He speaks.

- The Marine's in America have a God, Corp, Country hierarchy. In the church it's God, People, Society. In this country, it's just mates. No God. No Country. No Society. No People. Just mates. I'd like to think I made decisions throughout my life for the right reasons. As you get older, every decision you made in your youth seems to be the wrong decision. How are you supposed to know that then? But we are where we are. And I chose to look out for my mates. Does that make me a bad person or a person who made bad decisions? I don't ask for your forgiveness. Or the law's. I don't' ask for the church's forgiveness. I don't ask for society's forgiveness. I ask for God's. As I have my whole life. And will in whatever afterlife I receive. The Circles. That group of which you ask is not a church only group. There are business leaders. Arts leaders. Sports leaders. Political leaders. You can rip the band-aid off but I'm sure you will be told to put a new one back. This wound, this injury, this disease, affects all cultures and in this case it's bigger than our lives. I will give you the name you request. But once spoken I shall never speak that name again. And once spoken make of it what you will. And use it how you will. Yet, remember this, the snake's head will grow back. It's not called the Circle's because it starts and stops. It's the Circles because it goes around and around. When you realise how powerless you are to stop it, you simply contribute to it spinning in the hope it spins out of control and out of shape.

Grayson pauses. Then with little to no emotion says two words.

- Clarkson Glennis.

Grayson takes a longer pause. He makes the sign of the cross: forehead to chest and left shoulder to right shoulder. Looks at Natalie and I. Gently smiles and before we can react. Says - O' forgive me Lord. Before we can yell out no. Before we have time to blink. Grayson Bell pulls a handgun out from under his robe. Puts the gun to his temple.

And then Grayson Bell pulls the trigger.

Both myself and Natalie take a step back in shock.

Natalie pulls a pen out her pocket. Walks over to where the shell casing landed and picks it up. She looks at it, says - .40. Just like Chad.

I say - Are we thinking that Grayson shot Chad?

Natalie says - No.

- Are we thinking whoever shot Chad then came here and gave Grayson the gun with some explicit instructions?

- Yes.

I get my phone out and call the station to send a forensic team over.

It's been a busy day for them.

I say - Are we thinking Clarkson Glennis is next on the list of people with whom to speak?

Natalie says - Yes.

We wait for the forensics to arrive. While we wait I outline our next steps we will tell Rawls.

There aren't any arguments.

I say - As soon as the forensics arrive we're to go to Clarkson Glennis. There will be uniforms onsite to arrest Clarkson after we've had a talk.

It doesn't take long for the forensics to get to Grayson Bell's house. It seems as though people above Rawls' pay grade need this to be sorted quickly and quietly.

As the forensics walk in myself and Rita walk out.

We begin our drive to revisit Clarkson Glennis. Driving the other way are a series of news vans.

The longer the day goes the darker it gets.

Ebony Bowen

- What the fuck?, says Cary - How many more dead bodies are there going to be today?

More dead bodies? Who is it now? Where is it? I ask all these things to Cary.

- Yes more, Reverend Grayson Bell. I'm told he turned a gun onto himself. We have to go to his house. See what is going on.

Grayson Bell. This was unexpected. But why is he dead? Why would a church going man put a gun on himself? I thought that kind of thing was a sin in religious circles. Then it dawns on me. He was part of the Circles. If not part, then knew. Kept his mouth shut all these years. Someone tapped him on the shoulder and gave him a choice. Shame or sin. Grayson chose sin. I'm guessing the person who tapped him on the shoulder is the person who is behind all these murders. Perhaps even the person who has the missing child.

Find them, find the murder, and find the child.

Where to look?

We start driving on the road Grayson Bell's house is on. I see some cop cars drive the other way. I turn into the driveway and I see Grayson's house. Opulent. People don't live in houses like this without some serious coin in their pocket. If a religious man is capable of turning a gun on himself, then he is capable of holding onto some cash for his own purposes. Rather than give it to the poor like a good servant of God should, it probably got invested into property, shares, and other investment opportunities.

Religious ethics died right at the time the news media decided not to have any. For a career journalist, such as myself, this is hard to admit and harder to say out loud. Some of us try hard to present reality without bias. Editing, camera angles, colour corrections, and certain linguistic choices are designed to blur the lines between entertainment and life. Sometimes we get it wrong. Sometimes we get it right.

This story is one where we need to get it right.

I tell Cary - Pull the van over. I need to run something by you.

Cary pulls the van over, says - Grayson Bell's house is right there. What are we doing?

- Grayson Bell, what is a man like that doing living in a house like that?

- Probably enjoying his life. Who wouldn't want to live in a house like that in an area like this? Look around you Ebony, this place is a dream.

- Dream for Grayson. But no doubt, nightmares for other people. He is a church man Cary. What part of serving the will of God made him think this house was a good idea?

Cary stops. Looks around. Looks at the houses across the street. Crosses his face. He realises what the deal is here. He says - He knows some shady shit. Some Shady people. They held it against him. He didn't want to live in a house like this. He had to.

I nod my head.

Cary follows-up with - So who are the shady people holding it against him?

- Our murderer. Our kidnapper. This is all too convenient to be coincidental.

- Where do we find that person?

- We check what investments, properties or whatever Grayson has in his name. It is the only outlying lead that seems worth following. Let the other journalists find out Grayson's associates and background. Where he was this morning. What he had for lunch. What he did for the church. How much money he raised for charity. We need to call the fact-checkers at the station. Ask them to look into Grayson's investment portfolio. It'll have to be public for the position he had in society. He would have needed to disclose it. Justify it to the church and its practioners. They'll be a property listed. One that doesn't fit. One that was bought but not sold. Not used. Just bought and listed on an investment disclosure report. That'll be all the information there is on it. How much it got bought for and the address. All we need is the address.

Cary mulls it over. He nods in agreeance - Call the fact-checkers. Let's hope they can find something good.

I call them. There are a few rings before one of them answers.

- Hi, its Ebony Bowen. Do us a quick favour, look at the investments made by Reverend Grayson Bell for as far back as you can.

- Reverend?, says Virginia Cooper.

- Yes. Reverend.

- Hold on.

Virginia started her career as a fact-checker. Eventually did some good news reporting. Now, later in her career, went back to fact-checking. The reliability of a nine-to-five. We've talked. Had coffee, a few dinners, that kind of thing. Got some of the best advice about creating a news story from her.

I can hear her typing. There is some background noise. Talking. More typing. Laughter. A TV or radio is on. No music, just news. Other people in her office probably fact-checking other stories.

Thankless task really. Who decides what the facts are these days?
For every fact there is a claim of fake news.

- Well. Err, okay, Virginia says.

- Find something?, I ask.

- Yes, lots. What is it you are looking for? This guy had some
wealth. I didn't think church people had, or could have, this type of
investment.

- We're looking for an investment that was made but there is
really nothing else about it. A property was bought, not sold later for
profit while the real estate market is on an up. Just bought. That's it.
No refurbishment details. Nothing. Just bought. An amount and an
address. That's it.

- There is one. A house. In a sort of reasonable suburb. I wonder
why he'd buy there? It's hardly in the best suburbs in town lists. Not
in the bad lists either.

- Got an address?

Virginia gives me the address. I write it down. I show Cary who
nods and smiles. It's not far away.

- Thanks Virginia. We got to meet up again. See how things are
going.

She agrees and hangs up the phone.

I said I'd call Rita with any information we may have found. So I
do. I tell her the address I just got. I don't want to be a journalist
charged with obstruction of a police investigation. That's bad news
for any journalist let alone a crime reporter.

- Don't do anything stupid, she says.

- I won't.

Cary starts the van up and begins driving to our address.

There are moments in life when you make a choice that feels like you're riding a wave to a golden shore.

It's not until after do you realise you made a really bad choice.

I don't know it now, but this will be the worse choice I'll make in my life.

Yet, somehow, I won't be the one paying for the consequences.

Chapter 10

And I've done what I need to. I'm pretty sure I have. Well, I at least think I have. Whether or not I have, how can you be sure? There is one more person I can sort out but I won't. I'm going to let other systems take care of that person. If not a system then a process. If not a process then something else. If not something else then probably something else besides that. For people like that person, the public shame is far worse than what I would do. Public shame doesn't bother me. How can it? I don't exist. How does something bother what doesn't exist? How would it even try?

That's what I tell my friend. Who isn't doing anything. Has his legs pulled up to his chest with his arms wrapped around his legs. Like a little ball except a little person. Rocking back and forth. I ask him if he is hungry or thirsty. He says he wants to go home. He says he doesn't like this game. Which really annoys me because that is the same thing all my other friends said. When will kids ever start thinking for themselves?

I tell my new friend that he better get used to where he is because nothing is going to change. I tap on the door of his room with my crowbar. He keeps rocking back and forth. He tells me I'm horrible. Which would make me laugh if I could laugh but I can't. I tell him he reminds me of me when I was a little like him. He says no it doesn't because I'm horrible and he isn't. He asks me why I am like I am.

The comment hits hard. Even though I don't exist, sometimes things hurt. And this did. I think back to when I was little like him. I tell him bad people did bad things. I tell him I learnt that to beat bad you had to be badder. I tell him some other things. I'm not sure what they are. I tell him there is a video that shows why I am bad. He says he only wants to watch if it's a cartoon. I tell him I gave the video to someone. I pretended to be a courier. He says was it a cartoon? I say no.

I know what I'll show him I tell him. I get my phone out my pocket. I open the app that lets you see what the security cameras are showing. I click on the sample screen for the camera in this room. I show the phone and say look it's us watching us in a room watching us. He looks at the screen but it seems he can't quite figure it out. Or he did figure it out and just isn't that impressed. He says it would be better if it was a cartoon. I tell him I'm getting pretty fucking tired of him fucking carrying on about cartoons and that he should shut his fucking mouth before the crowbar I got shut's his fucking mouth for him. I show him the crowbar. He goes back to rocking back and forth. Which is far more tolerable than hearing about cartoons for the eighth time. Or tenth. Or some other number that can't be described by using a word.

Based on previous cycles such as the one I am in now. Around this time, I run out of patience. The cycle ends on purpose. A new cycle starts with purpose. This cycle is a bit different. Or it's the same. Maybe. I'm not going to explain the previous cycles so you can compare them with this. Or that. Or I really don't know anymore. Just be aware that the fuse is burnt out. The road ends. The path stops. The light goes dark. The sound becomes silence. Or any number of silly little sentences like that indicating an end. This sentence is a metaphor. This sentence is a simile. This sentence is just a sentence. I stand up. Look at my little friend. I say, time to bid thee farewell as thou is no longer impressed with thon's absurdity. My friend looks at me. Then he goes back to rocking back and forth.

At this point, dear reader, I'm going to let you imagine what happens. And something does happen. But that's up to you. Simply thinking nothing happens and all works out well is a most irresponsible approach. Something has to happen. The ending has already been written. But now, between you and me and our little friend here. What happens?

Before I can do any of that I look at the security cameras on the phone app. Much to my surprise. Or chagrin. Or pleasure. Or not. I see some movement just near the driveway of my house. It looks like one of them is holding a camera. The other one, I don't know who it is, isn't holding or carrying anything. They both seem to be looking at my house. If I had hairs on the back of neck I would feel them go up. My eyes widen. Or open further. A rush runs through my body. I get a tinge of excitement. Or apprehension. The end is near. Or a new beginning is near. Then they both stand up and walk closer to the front of my house. I press a button on my app and the front door opens just slightly. Just enough to tell someone that the door is open. Just enough to appeal to their curiosity to want to go inside. I pick up my crowbar and for good measure smash on the door of my friends little room and tell to politely shut the fuck up and stay that way.

I go and find a spot to hide. Or a spot where I won't be found. A spot where I can see my two new friends and watch what they do.

This is going to be good.

Natalie Fenix

Then there were three. Clarkson Glennis. The third person, who was probably the victim from yesterday and is on the DVD. And whoever has Mitchell Winters. Not sure who the kid in the video footage is but we passed it along to child services. Hopefully they might have a record or have someone on staff from back then who may recognise the kid. Clarkson Glennis may not have Mitchell but he sure as fuck knows who does. We should have pushed him harder earlier. But that darkness. Keeping its stinking claws in everything. Sowing the seeds of doubt and then watching them bloom. Making sure the light only goes so far and no further. It's a fine line. To balance asking questions against not raising suspicion. Its bad news when you ask one too many questions and the person shuts down. Or worse, they start asking for a lawyer.

Rita. Driving as usual. Not saying much. That DVD had some pretty fucked up shit going on. Answered some questions. Made you ask more. Those questions weren't getting answers. Her phone rings.

- Rita Allen, she says.

I can't make out what is being said but I can hear some words. Gun. Test. Same.

- You don't say, Rita says.

There is more talking on the other side of the call. Then Rita says - Okay, bye.

She looks at me and then back at the road then back at me.

- You're not going to believe this, she pauses then says - The gun Grayson Bell used to shoot himself is the same gun that was used to shoot Chad.

Seems redundant to say but I say it anyway - So who shot Chad and then gave Grayson the gun?

Rita smiles and says - Million dollar question isn't it. Let's hope Mr. Glennis here can give the answers we need.

- There is going to be some uniforms there to arrest Mr Glennis once we're done?, I ask.

- There will be, replies Rita.

We drive the rest of the way in silence. I think about my family. I think about what I've missed. What I'm missing. That familiar feeling rises in me. I take one look at the memory then push it back down. One look is all I can take at the moment. And in a few short minutes we pull up to Clarkson place. It's the same as before albeit with darker shadows. The uniforms are there waiting. One of them is opening and closing a pair of handcuffs. We nod at them. They nod back. I recognise one of them. The one who told me to come into the station yesterday.

We go inside the house. The same personal assistant notices and tries her best to stall us. I hear the words - Mr. Glennis is in a meeting at the moment and is not taking visitors.

We don't care. We walk by her.

She sees and jumps on the phone - They're back.

We open the door of Clarkson's office. He is sitting in his chair looking out the window. Back to us. He is definitely not in a meeting. The ice in the glass he's holding clinks as he turns to face us.

He says - Thought you'd be back sooner or later. I thought sooner.

It feels like he knew this moment was coming. He isn't surprised.

If anything, he is a little disappointed. He is wearing a suit and tie.
They aren't going to be worn again. At least not by him.

He turns back around goes back to looking out the window.

- Grayson Bell is deceased, states Rita.

- Yeah, how?

He stands up. Takes off his watch and puts in a draw in his desk.
Takes his mobile phone out his pocket. Puts it on the table. Takes
off his tie. Drapes it over the back of his chair. Takes off his belt.
Drapes it over the back of his chair next to his tie.

- Shot himself, I answer.

- Fuck, didn't think church going people had it in them. So you're
back. Got the Circle's figured out have you?

- Something else, says Rita.

- Yeah what?, Clarkson asks.

- A DVD was sent to a journalist who passed it on to us. It has
you on it, I say.

- With Grayson Bell and a third person. Had a bandage on their
arm, adds Rita.

Clarkson is expressionless so it's hard to describe what he looks
like. Let's just say concerned. He sits back down in his chair. He
knows full well what was on the DVD.

- Who is the kid?, asks Rita.

He takes a deep breath and shakes his head.

- Who is the other guy? The one who keeps hitting the chair the
kid is in with a crowbar. The one with the bandage on their arm?, I
ask.

Clarkson sighs and slumps a bit. He takes a breath. Pauses. Takes another breath. Goes to start talking but stops. He picks up the phone.

- Please call my lawyer.

He hangs up the phone. Look's at us, almost defiant but with an air of defeat, says - I will answer some questions and that's it. After that. Lawyer.

- The other guy, I say.

- Kid first, says Clarkson.

He keeps speaking.

- The kid. Do you know who this kid's parents are? Mum was a junkie. What the fuck was she doing taking a kid to an audition? She knew full well the kid wasn't getting a shot with a mother liker her. Overdosed years and years ago. Dad was a career criminal. Yeah, you've heard of him. Bank robbery. Violence. Guns. Knives. Abuser. Ask your boss about him. He arrested him and put him in jail for the rest of his life. Got killed in there a while back. Grayson took the kid in the day after that video was recorded. We considered him part of the Circle's but he never took part in anything like that again. Something switched in Grayson that day. Was never the same. Luckily we had plenty of stuff which incriminated him. So he kept his mouth shut. But where the circle ends is the same spot it starts again.

- Who is the child?, asks Rita.

- I don't remember their name's, says Clarkson - Jaxson or Jayden or something. One kid is the same as the other. Afterwards, Grayson set him up. Home schooled him. Gave him an allowance. Lives way off the grid. There'd be a birth certificate somewhere but that's it. No driver licence. No tax records. No social security number. Any financial thing went to Grayson. Grayson bought him a house, in Grayson's name of course. Only crossed paths with him once after that video was recorded. He couldn't quite put my face to the event but the look on his face. Every time I saw him. He wanted to visit some serious violence on me. Grayson had him on some type of leash.

Rita steps away from the conversation and makes a call. I over hear her.

- Check for properties in Grayson Bell's name.

Clarkson looks at me. He says - Looking for something are you?

I look at him - Looking for what?

- I remember you on the news years ago. Missing kid right?

- Yes. You know something about it?

- Not that one, Clarkson says.

I need to stay calm. I get this a little bit. Whenever I go to a restaurant or I'm out somewhere. There is occasionally someone who asks the same questions. I give Clarkson the same response as I give them people. I don't say or do anything.

Rita steps back to our conversation.

- How'd Grayson end up on the recording with you?

- I had similar footage of Grayson with another child.

- Where's that footage?

- With someone else.

- Who?

- You will never know. A circle is always closed. If a circle opens. Then it is just a curved line with a start and end. A circle is closed. Forever in a loop.

- Alright, who is the person with crowbar?, I ask.

Clarkson scoffs.

- Who is he?, Rita asks.

- I heard he died recently. I think it's time for the lawyer, says Clarkson.

- Is he the victim from yesterday morning?, I ask.

Clarkson scoff again, says one word - Lawyer.

- Fine, says Rita - So be it.

We leave. Rita's phone beeps.

- That beep is an address. Should be interesting.

On walking out of Clarkson's office I mention to the personal assistant - Be worried. Get a lawyer.

She stands there. Doesn't say a thing.

We get outside. Rita motions to the uniforms - Go inside and arrest Clarkson Glennis.

They do.

We get back in the car. Rita's phone rings.

- Don't do anything stupid, she says and ends the call.

- Don't do anything stupid? I say.

- Our journalist friend just gave me the same address we just got. Let's hope to hell we get there before she tries to get some story of year contender.

As we drive off I look at the shadows Clarkson's house makes.

They are not as dark as they were when we got here.

Ebony Bowen

We get to the house. I can't say if the address is going to pay off. The house is clean, neat and tidy. There is no grass. No trees. No shrubs. No plants, flowers or weeds. No leaves blowing around. The front of the house looks like a picture. A photograph. Static. Just an image no life. No story. No heart.

- Place looks dead, is this the right place?, says Cary.

I check the bit of paper I wrote the address on.

- Yep, right street, right number; right place, I say.

We both sit in the van looking at the house. Looking at its complete lack of identity. Of anything that suggests, well, anything. Thank fuck we have a camera to get a visual of the house. If I was writing for a paper there'd really be nothing to write that could explain this house. The nondescriptness of the house is a little awe inspiring.

- If you were some fucked up kidnapper of kids or serial killer you'd definitely want a house like this. There is absolutely nothing going for this house. No-one would give it a first look let alone a second look, says Cary.

We both pause. Without saying a word we get out the van and unlock the side door. Cary grabs a camera. I get the mic and sound recorder equipment. We check the gear. Then we pause again.

- Are we sure we want to go in? Should we wait for the police to get here?, I ask Cary.

- I can't see any other media vans here. This is our story. If the police were going to get here they'd be here by now. Let's just go knock on the door and see what happens, replies Cary.

I try to think of a reply but I got nothing. All journalists long for that one story where they're the first, and even better only, ones to get the story. I'd be stupid to fight it.

- What about the police? Would entering the house affect their ability to make arrests?, I ask just to be sure.

To the point but not in a harsh way Cary responds - No.

Cary puts the camera on his shoulder. He nods at me the way he usually does when we're recording. I walk towards the door. The house remaining as static as it was when we first arrived. The closer we get the more the front door looks slightly ajar. I don't where its coming from but there is a force trying to push me back. Stopping me from entering the house. Urging me to turn around and go back. If I knew how this was going to end now I would turn back but I don't. So I keep walking forward. I get to the front door. I don't knock. I pull on the door and open it a little further. Cary has the camera pointing into the house.

- It's too dark. I'm not getting anything. We have to go inside, goes Cary.

I take the first steps inside. It's dark but my eyes adjust and I can see some furniture. The inside as tidy as the outside. There is a TV on a stand. One lone chair facing the TV. Next to the chair is a small table. On it is the remote for the TV. There are no pictures on the wall. I keep walking forward. Cary has turned the light on the camera on and I can see a hallway which we start walking down. Step by step. It's more of a shuffle. Each step I take forward I get a strong feeling to take two back. We get to room off the hallway. It's the kitchen. There is a table with some seats around it. There is a faint smell of bleach. There are no dishes out. We walk out the kitchen and move further down the hallway. We get to next doorway. It's the last before the hallway ends in what has to be the laundry.

- Open the door, says Cary.

I grab the door handle and turn. But it doesn't open. I jiggle the handle and lean into the door to try to get it opened. It doesn't budge.

- It feels like it's locked from the inside, I say.

Cary kicks on the door a couple of times. Nothing happens.

- What now?, I ask.

There is a sound of a lock being unlocked. I turn the door handle again. The door opens. I open the door slowly waiting for whatever is on the other side to jump out.

Nothing jumps out.

I look at Cary and make the hand gesture to get behind me. He does and the light from the camera is aiming into the room. It looks like the room is full of dog kennels. Then I realise what they are. There are four small cages. Each cage door shut with a padlock. There are some coats and jumpers hanging off the wall. One of the coats is pink with a blue butterfly embroidered into the back. They look like children's clothes.

That little voice we all have in our heads, mine is screaming like a banshee. I don't listen. Something else is going on here. I crouch down and look into the small cage on the left. There is child lying down. Some dirt on his face. I'm sure it's a he. I wave Cary over and point. He aims the camera at the cage.

- Hello, I say - I'm Ebony. This is my colleague Cary. What's your name?

His small face looks at me. Emotionless. There are no smiles or frowns. Just a face looking. Then he covers his face with his hands. I turn around and standing behind Cary is a man holding what appears to be a large kitchen knife. A man with no hair. No eyelashes. No eyebrows. No beard or moustache. There is something familiar about him. Like I've seen him before.

It's the courier from earlier.

I breathe out in one of those ways when you realise something bad is about to happen and there is not a thing that can be done to change the outcome.

The light off the camera reflects off the knife. The motion was quick. Brutal. The blood drains from my face. Cary notices and drops the camera from his shoulder. He is about to say something but instead moans in pain.

The camera drops to the floor and Cary falls not long after.

The man points to the ceiling. I look up and I see a security camera.

I start to move towards Cary to see if he is alright.

The man says - Stay. Or don't move. Or some other adjective for not moving.

I don't listen and keep moving towards Cary.

The man slashes at my arm and cuts me good.

Cary moans and tries to get on his feet.

The man says - Get up and I will stab you again.

Then he kicks Cary in his side.

- Who are you says?, the man.

I point to the ID hanging around my neck. The man reaches out for it. I pass it to him.

- Fucking media, the man says followed by - Who sent you? Was it one of those stupid Circle conformist fucks?

- No-one sent us. I followed the leads and here we are, I respond.

- Police?, asks the man.

- Yes, we called them and gave an address. I get the feeling they found it themselves through Clarkson Glennis, I reply.

- Fuck that cunt. So where are the police?

- I have no idea.

The man looks at Cary. He says - I don't think he is going to be okay. If you don't want to be like him crawl backwards into the cage on the far right.

I turn around to look to see what cage. When I do the man grabs me by the hair a pushes me into the cage.

He screams - Get in the cage. Get in the cage. Get in the cage.

I try to fight back but it's pointless. The man has a handful of my hair and he guides, no, shoves me into a cage.

- Fuck, the man screams - Fucking adults.

- Who are you?, I ask.

- I don't know, says the man.

He gets a puzzled look across his face, asks - Did you not see the security cameras?

- No, I say.

The man smirks - Fucking media adults.

- Who are you?, I ask again.

- No-one. I don't even exist, says the man.

- Who's the kid?, I ask.

- My friend, says the man.

- Is it Mitchell Winters?, I ask.

- How the fuck do I know?, says the man - I mean. I don't know.

Or something. Could be I 'spose. If it isn't then it's someone else.

- Can you help my friend please?, I ask.

- No, says the man. He throws a rag at me.

I tie it around my arm to cover the gash. I notice there's far more blood than what should be. It drips down my arm, over my fingers, and pools on the floor. This is bad.

He drags Cary out the doorway. He picks up a crowbar and bangs on the cage where the kid is. He yells - See what happens. Do you? Fucking look.

The man points at Cary.

The kid crawls up into a ball. He doesn't scream. Doesn't cry. Just looks straight ahead and blinks.

The man leans the crowbar next to the doorway. He shuts the door and it is pitch black.

Those voices in my head have stopped. There is no force pushing or pulling at me. Like the house itself, the cage I am in is static.

The smell of my blood becomes noticeable. I feel the wetness of the rag. It must be soaked in blood. I take my belt off and strap it around my arm. I can feel some numbness in my fingers. I can feel my heart rate is elevated.

I'm in trouble here. The police better get here soon.

I didn't think total darkness would be this fucking scary.

I can't imagine what Mitchell Winters, if it is Mitchell Winters, is going through.

Chapter 11

I know reader, I should've told you about the security camera back
when I was telling you about my house. But you're the reader. Mr or
Ms or Mx Smarty-pants. Or superstar. Or the author that is alive.
Or something else where I'm just not sure what. It's not like I can
give you an actual tour of my house so you can see for yourself. I
don't exist. If I don't exist then my house doesn't exist. If my house
doesn't exist then I can't tell you, or show if you want to be the
literary genius which I'm sure you do, that my house has camera's
setup. I can't advise that I can see people walking up the driveway. I
can't advise that I can watch people as they make their way around
my house. I can't advise that I can pick my moments. But so you
know, I can see people walking up the driveway. If they get inside
the house and I can watch where they go and what they do. I can
pick my moment. Right now my moment is to let them get in the
house and make their way to the room where my friend is. Once
they open the door the shock of what they see will leave them
momentarily (that's a big word) stunned (which is also a big word).
At that moment I will strike. The plan worked for the media person
and the cameraman it should work this time around as well.

You know what people say if they said stuff.

I thought the media person. Ebony, that's her name. I've seen her on
TV a few times. Never seen her in real life though. Makes me
wonder if she even exists. I know I don't. I thought Ebony said she
called someone to let them know where she is. Based on what I'm
watching on the monitor now, she called the police. They look like

police. Not uniformed police. The other ones. The ones you see on TV. I think they're called detectives. I'm sure I've heard people call them that. As far as name calling goes, it's a fairly nice name.

This is getting stranger.

How the hell can they be here if I don't exist?

Guess my existential crisis was real.

I think about moving the cameraman from out of the kitchen. Then I don't think about moving the cameraman from out the kitchen. Ebony is with my new friend. By the looks of what I'm watching I'm going to have a couple new friends soon.

I see one get out of the police car. They run to the media van up while crouching. They open the van door, look around and then run back to the police car. I have a button I can press that unlocks the front door leaving it slightly ajar. I'm certain I've already mentioned that. If not, I'm mentioning it now. I press the button. Or switch. Or lever. Or something.

The police get out their car and walk up the driveway. There are two of them. As they get closer I see that they are both female police. They walk slowly. Step by step. They stop at the front door. There are a few hand gestures. One counts down from five using their hand. One of them kicks the door open. I can hear the kick. It's weird watching someone kick a door on a TV but hearing the very thing in real life. I feel a little disassociated. Like I don't exist and this is all just being made up on the fly.

I leave the room and go to where my friends are. Ebony says things like please mister let us leave. Or, just let the kid go and take me. Or something else.

I pick up the crowbar and bang on the little rooms they are in. Neither of my friends scream or shout. They just move back as far as they can away from where I'm hitting with the crowbar. I leave the room and as I'm leaving I hear Ebony say please mister again. I don't respond. I just shut the door and lock it. I can see some shadows where my front door is. It seems both police people are inside my house. My domain. My home ground. My advantage. My whatever you want to make up.

I make my way out of the room where my friends are. The police will need to look in that room before they move forward. They will notice the cameraman near the table. I can hear some gurgling or bubbling like sound. There is a clearish liquid tinged with red dripping from the corner of the cameraman's mouth. I've seen worse. Heard worse as well.

For someone with no eyes or ears being able to see and hear is almost a miracle.

I see the police get to the door. They stop. One of them points to the cameraman and crawls up to them. They check the cameraman's pulse. Shake their head no. The other one points to a door. They try to turn the handle. It's locked. I smile. I know it's locked. I locked it. I open my smartphone and unlock the door. The two police look at each other. They heard the door unlocked. They open the door and as they do I activate the lights in the room. They are fluorescent for a purpose. It's to create a blinding effect.

There is a voice. It's Ebony's. The voice says hey, pigs, you pig fucking pigs, get me the fuck out of here.

Both the police stumble into the room. Rubbing their eyes. Trying to acclimatise their eyes to the new situation.

One of the police says wait, I can't see for shit.

Waiting is giving me more time to react. Which works for me. I won't complain because if I do the police will know where I am and I don't want them to know where I am.

Ebony speaks again and says please get me the fuck out of here.

One of the police says Ebony fucking Bowen?

Ebony says no shit. Now get me the fuck out of here.

The other police officer says shut the fuck up bitch and wait a bit. We're going to get you out. Just hang the fuck on.

Cary. Have you seen Cary the fucking using back stabbing worthless piece of shit? Ebony asks.

Cary must be the name of the cameraman. Or the name of someone else. But I don't know why someone would be talking about someone who isn't here.

There is some silence. I leave where I'm crouched and move slowly closer to the room the police and my friends are in.
Ebony talks again. Open this fucking door. Use the fucking crowbar next to the door. Anyone right minded person would think you pig fuckers have never opened a door before.

There is some noise. Something breaks. It must be the padlock on the door.

About fucking time. Don't forget the little fucker in the other cage says Ebony.

One of the police says what little fucker?

Stupid little piece of shit hasn't said anything since I been here. Makes you wonder what kids at school are being taught these days says Ebony.

Fuck, that little fucker is Mitchell Winters says one of the police.

I hear some more banging and breaking.

Hang on you little fucker says the police.

Who the fuck are you pig fuckers? Mitchell says.

Watch your mouth you little fucking piece of shit says the police.

Did those oedipal pieces of shits I have to call Mum and Dad send you? Mitchell asks.

Yes they fucking did. Wouldn't shut the fuck up when you first went missing says one of the police. They were all boo fucking who and shit. We were all like shut the fuck up you whiny fucks. Let us do our fucking jobs and we'll see if we can find that little fucker.

How many times do I have to say hurry the fuck up? asks Ebony.

Sounds like the padlock on Mitchell's cage just got broke off. Mitchell must be a bit hesitant to leave. Perhaps he likes it here.

I hear one of the police say those whining bitch of parents of yours are out the front. Now get out here you little fuck. Just grab my fucking hand and let's get the fuck out of here.

That is word for word exactly how the conversation between those people went. If it wasn't word for word, then it was at least other words for other words. If it wasn't between those people, then it was at least between other people. But that conversation happened. Or it happened another way. Or it didn't happen at all and I just made it up. Or someone else made it up but why would they do that? Or something else. Real life has much to answer for. Problem is nobody is asking it any questions. I would but I don't exist so I can't ask it any questions. Or, whatever, does it really matter anymore?

I see Ebony leave the room. She is holding Mitchell in her arms. Screaming. One of the police is pushing the other police. Who has a blank look on her face. Like she's seen a ghost. Or a monster. Or whatever bullshit is in horror movies these days. Or something else. Or worse.

There is a flickering of red and blue lights against the walls. I see Ebony go out the front door. Then one of the police people turn arounds and sees me standing behind the other police person. They throw up. It's just bile and spit.

I say you fucking cunt. Or cunt. Or some other version of cunt. I hate vomit in my house. It's bad enough cleaning other people's vomit.

Then I bring the knife down across the body of the police person I'm standing near.

Natalie Fenix

We stop in front of the house. There is a news van parked out the front and another one, which looks like a thousand others, is in the driveway.

- She better not've gone inside, says Rita - I swear to fuck if she has I'll lock her in a cell back at the station.

I look around to see if there is anyone around. I don't see anyone.

- Maybe they are in the back of the van getting the camera ready for a live news cross.

- She'd fucking want to be there.

We look around sizing up the area. There is a familiarity with this place but strange at the same time. It looks like any low socio-economic area. Some houses where people have given up. Maybe given up is the wrong term. More realised the futility of their situation. However, like any place on earth, there is a dichotomy at play. Right next door is a house where people are trying their hardest the keep there heads above water. Most times the water keeps rising and people end up letting the water rise above their heads. The next door house looks like they are hanging on for dear life.

We focus on our house.

- Does this place look weird to you?, asks Rita.

- Don't know. Yes but no as well. Looks like any house with a modicum of effort put into keeping the place tidy.

- Yeah, but. Where is the life? The place just looks like a picture. A copy of a picture which was a copy of another picture. It's like looking at a darkened tunnel but you can only see the first couple of metres and after that the darkness is too dark to see any further.

She makes a good point. The longer I look at the house, I start to see what Rita might be drawing my attention towards. No grass. No trees. No life. No soul. The house is lifeless. You wouldn't think twice about the house. You'd just keep walking or driving by oblivious to its existence.

Rita says - I better go check to see if Ebony is in the back of their news van. Back in a sec.

Rita gets out the car. She does that walk where people keep low to try to hide themselves from sight. It looks funny when there is nothing to duck behind. She opens the van door and her shoulders slump. She runs back to our car and gets back in.

- No-one there, goes Rita.

- They go inside the house?

- Not sure. I hope not. They better have not.

- What about the other van in the driveway? Want me to run the plates?, I ask Rita?

- Yeah, sure. Why not?, she replies.

I punch the letters and numbers in our Mobile Data Terminal. After a few seconds a result appears. If I had a mouthful of water I'd spit it out.

- Van is registered, I say.

- Yeah, who?, Rita asks.

- Grayson Bell.

Rita sighs - I think we're where supposed to be.

We both look at the house. The front door is slightly ajar. There is a flicker of light and what sounds like someone banging on a piece of steel. I reach for the gun in my holster and load it ready. Rita does the same.

- How far away is everyone else?, I ask.

Rita goes - Rawls said they'd be here as soon as possible. Could be about to turn the corner. Could still be at the station going through a plan. We better go in. Follow me.

We get out the car. Rita takes the lead. The darkness that speaks to me asking questions over and over has stopped. It's not asking anything. It watches. Waiting for something to unfold. Like it's in a win-win situation. Either way is a result the darkness will be comfortable with. It feels as though there is an ending nearby. Yet evading. Keeping out of sight. Trying not to give the game away. Keeping the good stuff for itself. That is the thought that terrifies me. Ready to raise its hand to answer whatever question is asked.

We get to the front door. Rita peaks inside. She points at her eyes and shakes her head no and points at me. I peak through the slight gap with between door and frame. I point at my eyes and shake my head no. Rita holds her hand up showing a five and pulls down her thumb.

Four.

Then her fingers.

Three.

Two.

One.

Rita kicks the door open and steps inside pointing her gun to the left. I follow right behind her pointing my gun to the right. After a moment our eyes adjust to the darkness. There is a single seat facing a TV. Nothing on the walls. We both pause. Listening. Waiting for something to happen to guide our next steps. Nothing happens. I look at Rita who motions to move forward down the hall.

We get to the end of the hall and Rita puts her hand up to stop. Then she motions to come closer and points. On a table there is a camera. The kind the media use. Facing us. I can't tell if it's recording. On the floor someone is lying there. There is a blood stain on his shirt on his lower back. There is a small pool of blood on the ground where the wound has been dripping. Rita couches down low and checks his pulse. She looks at me. Shakes her head no.

I turn around and see a door. It's closed. I get Rita's attention. She nods. I turn on the door handle. Door is locked. I turn on the handle again and lean into the door. It won't open. I take a step back.

I hear a click as though the door has been unlocked from the inside. As soon as we get in the room the lights turn on. They are fluorescent. They are blinding. I hear a voice. It's a female voice.

- Get me out of here, the voice says.

My eyes struggle to get focus. Those spots you get when you look at a bright light still impede my vision. I reach out to see if there is something I can grab hold of to keep my balance. There is nothing.

- Wait, I can't see, I say.

The voice pleads - Please get me out of here.

My vision starts to return. I see the female voice. Looks terrified but familiar. I see other small cages in the room. I focus on the female voice.

- Ebony Bowen, I state.

- Yes. Please let me out, Ebony says.

Rita goes - Hang on Ebony. We'll get you out. Just hang on a second.

- Cary. Have you seen Cary?, Ebony asks.

I don't say anything.

Cary must be the person we just passed.

I lie.

- No, you're the first person we've seen.

Rita doesn't say anything.

- The camera's. He is watching, Ebony says while pointing to the ceiling.

- Fuck, says Rita.

She turns around. Watching our backs. I try to figure to a way to open the door.

- Open the door. Use the crowbar next to the door, says Ebony.

I see the crowbar. It has blood stains on it. I know its evidence but I don't think twice to use it to pry open the padlock. It eventually gives. I grab Ebony's hand and pull her out the cage.

- Don't forget the kid, says Ebony.

Rita turns around - The kid?

- Hasn't said anything since I've been locked in there, says Ebony.

She points to another cage. In it is a child.

- That's Mitchell Winters, says Rita.

I use the crowbar to pry open the padlock on Mitchell's cage.

His eyes widen when he sees the crowbar. He covers his face with his hands and screams.

- Hang on Mitchell, I say - hang on.

I can't get the padlock open quick enough.

- Who are you? Mitchell says.

- The police buddy, I say - the police.

- Did Mum and Dad send you?, Mitchell asks.

- Yes, they can't wait to see you, I say.

I'm trying to keep Mitchell calm. And myself. Those cameras have spooked me. Someone is watching us meaning they are probably a step ahead. Which I don't like one bit.

- Hurry up, begs Ebony.

I get the padlock off and open the cage door. I reach in to get Mitchell.

He kicks out at me and says - No.

I say - Mitchell, just take my hand. It'll be ok. Mum and Dad are just out the front.

They're not but I'll say just about anything to get Mitchell out the cage.

- C'mon Mitchell. Just take my hand, I say again.

Mitchell begins to cry and takes my hand. I grab him up, stand up and see something I never thought I'd see again. My ears start to ring. I hug Mitchell a little tighter. Then that memory I try to supress surges out. I can't help it. That smiling face smothers my mind's eye. That playful giggle when kids are being naughty but knowing they won't get in trouble because they are just having fun drowns out the ringing. I turn to face Rita whose mouth is moving but I can't hear a thing. I feel like I'm in the middle of a cyclone. That calm that happens between the first and last moments of a storm. She has seen the coat as well. The pink coat with the blue butterfly embroidered into the back. Rita takes Mitchell from me and passes him to Ebony. She points to go outside. I stand there and look back at the pink coat. There are other coats hanging on the same wall. They all look like children's coats. I dry reach a couple of times. Rita grabs my shoulder and pushes me out the room. I get out the room and Ebony is standing there looking at the body under the table in the kitchen. I can't hear but it looks like she is screaming. I grab her spare hand and pull her away. Rita is pushing at me to get out the house. I keep hold of Ebony's hand. I can feel her legs wanting to give way but I grasp her hand tighter and pull her with me. I turn around to see where Rita is and right behind her is a tallish hairless man. I try to say something to warn her but that memory is in control. All I can see is that small angelic face. Hair drooping over her eyes. I want to reach out and push it behind her ears but there is no point. It's just a memory. Behind the memory I see the hand of the tallish hairless man reach out over Rita mouth and it pulls her backward. A look of pain crosses Rita's face. Her mouth looks like it screamed but I couldn't hear. I let go of Ebony's hand and push her outside with Mitchell. I see blue and red light flickering against the wall of the front room. Then my memory speaks. It will be the last words the memory says to me.

It says - Do it Mom. You'll be okay. Do it.

The tallish hairless man says - You fucking cunt. Or something.

I say - Let her go.

I don't hear it. I just feel my mouth move to make those sounds.

Rita is saying something but I can't hear. It looks like she is saying - Get out. Just go.

I go back to the memory. The memory smiles.

It is the most beautiful smile I've ever seen.

The memory waves, giggles then turns around and runs off. I can hear laughter as the memory fades. As it fades the reality of this situation comes fully into focus. I take a deep breath. I feel like I've slept for three days straight. There is no tiredness. No aches in my joints or fatigue in my muscles. I feel re-charged. My breathing feels great. I look at Rita.

She is yelling at me - Get out.

I shake my head no. The tallish hairless man brings a knife from above Rita's head and tries to stab her. As he is bringing the knife down I lunge forward and knock his hand. It gashes Rita's arm. She screams in pain and the tallish hairless man lets her go.

Blood drips onto the floor.

- You stupid fuck. What was coming to this cunt is now coming for you, goes the tallish hairless man.

Rita has fallen forward away from the tallish hairless man. I grab her and tell her to go outside.

- Don't do anything you shouldn't, Rita says.

- I'm going to hurt you fuckers something bad. Or something, goes the tallish hairless man.

- Fine, I say - do your worst, there is no way someone like you has anything resembling good.

The tallish hairless man scoffs - We'll see. Who the fuck are you and how did you find this place?

I point into the room Mitchell and Ebony were in.

I say - That pink coat hanging on the wall. That was my daughter's. She went missing eight years ago.

The tallish hairless man goes - I just got her. Or him. I just get them. Other people do the bad stuff.

I ask - Who are you, what's your name?

The tallish hairless man says - I don't know who I am. I don't even exist which is so weird you're here. How can you be here if I don't exist? Was it those stupid Circle Conformist Fucks? Which one of them gave me up? Trenchie? Chad? If it was Trenchie then fuck that fuckwit. Stupid prick couldn't count to three even if he had a calculator to help him. The less we say about Chad the better.

Not that I'll say but he is spot on about them two so instead I say - They're both dead.

- I know that, says the tallish hairless man.

He has one of those condescending looks people get when they think they are out smarting you.

Then he says - It couldn't have been Grayson Bell I made sure he wasn't going to speak.

I let the tallish hairless man keep talking.

- Wait. I know how. My fingerprints were on file, the tallish hairless man says.

Then he cracks up laughing and holds up his hands. There are bandaids on each of his fingers and thumbs.

The tallish hairless man goes - I burnt them off. Or whatever the words for burning something off are.

- Clarkson Glennis mentioned some investments Grayson Bell made, I say.

The tallish hairless man stops.

- Told me some things. Not your name though, I say.

- I don't exist so I can't have a name, the tallish hairless man says. He looks down at my hand.

- Saw a DVD. Know anything about that?

- Yes, the DVD. I know who the kid is.

- Who? We know who the three adults on the DVD are, but not the kid.

- Me.

- Me?

- Yes, me, I'm the kid. Or I'm another kid somewhere else.

- You?

- Yes. Me. Fuck that day. Grayson took me under his wing. Gave me this house. I got some kind of life. If you can even call it life. But the other day. When I saw that fuck with the crowbar. The scar on his arm. Something happened inside. Something ended. I couldn't see anything after that. No colours. No shapes. No events.

I look at my hand which is holding a gun. I forgot about the gun. I look back at the tallish hairless man.

- Go on. Use it.

I keep the gun by my side. I don't raise it.

- When we're finished here I 'm going to do something I should have done at the start, says the tallish hairless man.

- Which is? I ask.

- Kill Clarkson Glennis.

- I'm going to cut to the chase, I say - We have already arrested him. Now, you are under arrest for suspicion of kidnapping. You may receive other charges as relevant evidence is gathered. You don't have to do or say anything. If you do it may be used as evidence against you. You should give your name and address when asked. You should speak to a lawyer first before answering any other questions. Do you understand?

The tallish hairless man says - Already arrested him? They'll get him in prison. People like him are marked on day one. They don't make day two. Don't you think you should consider that before coming to conclusions?

- No, I say.

A confused look draws across the tallish hairless man's face. He looks at the ground. I see what he is looking at.

I say - Do not pick that up.

I raise my gun and point it at the tallish hairless man.

He looks at me then the knife and then back at me.

- Don't so it, I say again.

- Do what you must. I don't exist so it doesn't matter anyway, says the tallish hairless man.

He crouches down and picks up the knife. As he is standing back up I pull the trigger. The wall behind him covers in blood. The tallish hairless man stands there trying to figure it out. He looks at me, lifts the knife and takes a step forward.

I unload my clip into him. He falls and hits the ground. A blank look across his face. Eyes open.

It's the first person I've ever shot. It will be the last.

Someone outside on a megaphone says - Put the guns down we are coming inside.

I kneel down and put the gun down in front of me. I hear steps of police boots trample into the house.

- Clear, a police person says.

- Clear, says another.

- In here. Get a paramedic. Get two, I tell them.

Neither are for me.

Rawls walks in says - Are we good here?

One of the police officers says - Yes.

- Get her out. Get everyone in here. Get that kid to the hospital. Call his parents tell them. Get the police lawyer here as well.

Rawls pauses.

Then he says - And keep the fucking media away from here until

I fucking say so.

I reach for that memory. I search for it. But it's gone. Now I have this warm feeling. It's comforting. I feel someone's hand under my arm lifting me up. I look and it's Rawls.

- Come on, Rawls says - let's get out here.

I shake loose and go into the room where the cages are. I grab the pink coat with the blue butterfly embroidered into the back. I walk back out. Rawls see's the coat.

- You can't remove evidence, you know that, he says.

- Leave her, Rita says leaning against the wall.

Rawls realises whose the coat is then says - Okay, get out of here, go.

I walk out the front of the house. I see Mitchell and Ebony being looked over by a paramedic. Ebony has her arms around Mitchell who is hugging her back. Ebony looks up and sees me. She smiles and rests her chin on top of Mitchell's head. I nod. Another paramedic grabs me and leads me to the back of another ambulance. He passes me a bottle of water. I undo the top and take a large mouthful. I tip the rest over my face. I sit in the back of the ambulance. Head in my hands waiting for the inevitable. But it doesn't happen. I saw my memory smile and as much as I want her here now, seeing the smile brings a certain relief.

I look around at the sea of people. Forensics. Other detectives. Paramedics. Junior officers keeping people behind the crime scene tape. Some journalists stand behind the tape. Holding their microphones out. Asking for comments. Asking questions. Some jot down notes on a notepad. Everyone trying to do their jobs as best they can. A system keeping everyone in line. I look at the people.

The dark is gone. There is light emanating from everyone. I see some people. My gaze fixes on them. I see her. My daughter. My heart skips a beat. My husband crouches down beside her and points in my direction. My daughter sees me. Her eyes widen with joy. A mixture of laughing and smiling contorts her face. She runs at me arms wide.

- Mummy, she screams.

My husband just steps behind her.

I crouch down and open my arms. My daughter leaps into them and nearly knocks me over.

- I missed you so much Mummy, she says.

I hug her like it's the last time I will. I vow to myself from here on to hug her every time like it's the last. My husband walks to us. I reach out to hug him as well. He smiles and hugs us back. It's the safest I've felt for a long time. I show him the pink rain coat under my arm. He looks at it. Then at me. A tear drops from his eye. He hugs me.

He says - Thank you. I want her back so bad.

I say - I do to.

I lean up to kiss him. There is tension. The things I've missed. Not said. Avoided. Rescheduled. Declined. It has all got to add up. We have a lot to talk about. Which is exactly what my husband says.

I say - I know.

My husband kisses back.

It's the best I've felt for a long time.

Rawls walks over - Go home rest.

- You sure. Need me to put something on paper?

- No. Go home, says Rawls. He walks off.

- Let's go home, I say.

My daughter says - Yay, I can show Mummy all my school stuff.

I smile.

My husband says - That was a fun time getting that together. Geez.

- I wish I was there. I've missed so much.

A few steps away, Rawls turns around and yells - Back to the station tomorrow to answer some questions. Get your's and Rita's story together.

I nod. I will do all that. But right now, I need home. My family. My shower. My bed.

My husband.

9

The phone rang. It rang a few times. David thought it might be Annie's parents letting them know how far away they were. David picked up the phone.

- Hello?

He couldn't quite understand at first. Just heard the fragments of what was being said. A man. A house. People hurt. Police injured. Investigation starting.

Then the voice said - We have found Mitchell.

David said - Hang on a second. What?

The voice started again. Spoke clearly. Slightly slower than before - Mitchell has been found. Several people have been killed. Several others, including a police officer, have been injured. A house has been sequestered for further investigation. Detectives at the scene are continuing their investigation.

The police officer told David to get a pen. David did. He wrote down the ward and room number of the hospital Mitchell was being monitored in. David looked at Annie. Not quite sure how to tell her. Annie looked back. The world stopped. Not just one of those pauses where you take a moment but time keeps going. The world. Time. The whole universe. Everything. It stopped. Just for a second.

A second was enough.

David told Annie.

Whatever weight was Annie shoulders disappeared in an instant.

Grief. Gone.

Shock. Gone.

Trepidation. Gone.

Despair. Gone.

Replaced with more positive emotions and thoughts.

Joy.

Pleasure.

Happiness.

Relief.

Bekka was there to. Her hand grasping Annie's. Bekka could feel all that weight leave. She looked at her sister. Bekka had never seen her so, so, so, well she couldn't think up the word she needed.

Annie let go of her sister's hand and wrapped her arms around David. She almost suffocated him. Bekka stood up. After a moment Annie saw her standing. Both she and David grabbed her and pulled her into their hug. Annie cried. Bekka did to. David tried to hold it together.

He couldn't.

For the next five minutes the three of them stood arm in arm. Tears of joy. Of exhaustion. Of happiness.

Then the situation cleared up. What the hell were they doing standing here hugging each other? There weren't time for showers or brushing teeth. Bekka ran her hand through her hair to straighten it out. Annie pulled her hair into a pony tail. David put on a hat. David grabbed the car keys. The car started and they were driving to the hospital. No need to warm the car up. Seatbelts were on while they were backing out the driveway. Mint flavoured chewing gum passed around. Bekka realised she or Annie had better tell their parents. They were going to show up at Annie's house any minute. Bekka called them. Told them to go straight to the hospital instead.

The hospital was a thirty minute drive. The car radio stayed off. David drove. Not taking his eyes off the road. Bekka looked out the window at the buildings going by. At other cars. At the trees blowing in the breeze. Annie chewed on her fingernails. She looked over at the speedometer.

It said 60.

Can't the speed limit go any quicker? Hurry up Annie silently urged. She could see the top of the hospital in the nearby distance.

They finally got there. David pulled up to the kerb in a nearby street. Didn't even bother straightening the car parking. Just stopped the car. Put it in park. All three were out the car at the same time. Not running but they got into the hospital. They looked for signs to the ward Mitchell was in. This way. Turn left. That way. Up some stairs. Turn left again. Down the corridor. They made it to the ward.

The desk nurse looked at them. She knew right away.

- Mitchell Warner?, she asked.

Annie and David, at the same time, said - Yes.

The desk nurse pointed down the hall - Second on the right.

Annie leapt ahead and went straight to the room. She turned in and saw Mitchell sitting on the bed. Mitchell burst out in tears and ran to Annie. She picked him up. Told him it's all going to be oaky. David walked in the room. Saw Annie holding Mitchell. Smiled. Mitchell saw his Dad. He reached over and hugged him as well.

Bekka looked around the room. She recognised Ebony Bowen from the news. She was sitting in a seat alongside someone else. Both were getting their arms seen to by a nurse. It looked like they were getting stitches.

Rita held out her hand.

- Hi, I'm Detective Rita Allen. Tough kid here, she nodded

towards Mitchell.

- I'm Bekka, Annie's sister.

The shook hands.

The nurse finished with Rita and said - Keep that wound clean. Take these antibiotics once a day after food. Let us know if you feel any pain or if the wound gets infected.

- Yep, said Rita - my kids are going love seeing this scar. She looked at Annie and David - We have some questions, but they are for tomorrow. Now. Get some rest. Spend some time with Mitchell. Make sure he gets some rest, said Rita. She got up - I'm home then. I don't know how I'm going to explain this to my husband.

Mitchell spoke - Thanks for helping me Mrs. Policeman.

Rita smiled - All good young man. Can you do one thing for me? Mitchell nodded.

- When your parents tell you to clean your room; clean your room.

Mitchell smirked and sunk back into the warm embrace of his Mum.

Just before Rita got to the doorway, Annie said - Thank you.

David nodded in agreement.

Rita smiled and left.

Bekka looked over to Ebony. She looked like she'd been through an ordeal herself. A large cut on her arm being sewn shut.

- Here for the story?, Bekka asked.

Ebony looked at Bekka, shook her head no - Not right now I'm not. Ebony pointed to her arm then a nearby table, - Felt much worse about an hour ago. The wetness of the rag sure seemed like a lot of blood was being lost.

Bekka looked over. The rag was a red. Glossy but dark, - What the hell happened in that house?

- I'm not sure. Found a child. Saw my life flash before my eyes. Lost a friend, not sure how I can explain that. Looks like I'll be the news for a bit instead of writing it. How do you explain any of this to anyone?

Bekka didn't have an answer. She put her hand on Ebony's shoulder. Ebony just sat there and stared at the floor piecing together the series of events. She hoped she could remember each moment.

The nurse finished sewing Ebony's wound closed then gave the same line to Ebony as she had with Rita.

Bekka caught Mitchell's eye. He smiled resting his head on Annie's shoulder. He looked tired. He looked like he was about to go to sleep.

Mitchell would have to wait.

Annie and David were going to kiss him a thousand times. Mitchell wasn't to going fight it. He would take all those kisses if it meant he'd never have to go back to that house. Even though his Auntie Bekka had slobbery auntie kisses. He would take all those as well. He would keep his room tidy. He would eat all his dinner. He would play nice with his friends. He wouldn't get his brand new clothes dirty so Mum didn't have to wash them all the time. He would help his Dad in the garden. Even though he didn't know how, he would mow the lawn so he could play outside. He would take the rubbish out. He wouldn't draw on the walls anymore. And he would brush his teeth before going to bed without needing to be asked.

Mitchell would do all those things.

Just as long as he never had to go back to that house. Have to talk to that weird man who thought he saw a giraffe pretending to be a cat.

Just as long as never had to do any of that.

Ever.

Acknowledgements

Family. Friends. Colleagues. Peers. - Thank you.